A.L.U

Artificial

Life

Universe

(signature: GROSOIU MARIAN)

Marian Grosoiu

(signature)

Dear reader,

I thought it would be easier to connect with this book if I told you a little bit about myself and the reason I wrote this book in the first place.

So, hello, I am Marian. I am the co-owner and chef of a lovely Italian restaurant, called Rustico, located in Bury St. Edmunds, United Kingdom.

You're probably asking yourself how I came to write this book, and this is the reason I would hope people get close with it and its characters. Some time ago, I was in a car accident. Nothing was damaged physically, besides the car I was driving at the time, but I entered a dark period mentally. My thoughts were clouded, my focus gone. I felt as if I couldn't do anything right anymore and as if I was letting the people around me down, because I couldn't be the best version of myself. What was worse though were my sleepless nights. The walls and ceiling were my entertainment for a long period of time. This is when I discovered my imagination. I started creating scenarios in my head, sometimes even whole movies, and I realized they were helping me fall asleep when thoughts were in control of my mind. These stories that took place in my head went on for a while, until one day, when I created Robert's character.

Robert was made in my image. However, I created him to be my better self. He is what I would be if I had the possibilities. His character does for his family what I would want to be able to do if I was in his place. The rest of the characters came naturally to me.

Writing this story became my getaway. I wrote in the morning, during breaks, before going to sleep. Even during the night, there were times when I laid in bed 'writing' the story in my head, putting it on paper the next day.

It was scary in the beginning, I won't lie. I didn't know where to start, I had never done something like this, writing a book, but I had people around who encouraged me to keep going, even when I wasn't sure if what I was doing was right. It's those people, along with my ambition to not only show the world, but myself, that I CAN do it, who kept me going every day.

Table of Contents

Chapter 1

In the year 2100, somewhere in the United Kingdom, lived a family made up of a father, Robert, a mother, Emily, and their 7-year-old daughter, Emma. The mother worked as a teacher in a nearby school, while the father was an IT engineer.

One day, while the mother was at work, she started feeling ill, a pounding headache and dizziness taking over her. The schoolmistress called for an ambulance and, alarmed, announced Robert of what happened, telling him that the ambulance is taking his wife to the county hospital.

Asking his boss to leave work, he got in his car and, worried to the core, started driving to the hospital. On the way, he called his sister and begged her to pick up his daughter from school. After a one-hour-long drive, he arrived at the hospital, extremely concerned.

At the reception, he asked where his wife was taken. A minute later, a doctor came to talk to him about his wife's situation, finding out that she was seriously ill, being diagnosed with a rare disease. The doctor told him a professional would be with him shortly and the man sat down to wait for this doctor. He was feeling terrible, everything around him seemed to be demolishing, nothing made sense anymore. He felt as if he could not breathe properly, so he went outside to catch his breath, hoping to recover.

Shortly, the doctor came to ask the man to follow him into his office. There, the doctor offered him a coffee. However, the man said that coffee was not what he needed right now, but answers, regarding how his wife was.

"I want to see my wife!" he said, worried.

The doctor managed to calm him down and started to talk about his wife, confirming the diagnosis of the rare disease and announcing that she had gallen into a deep coma.

Desperate, the man started crying, ripping his hair out of his head, shocked by the news. The doctor hugged him, trying to calm him down once again.

"I need you to calm down in order to be able to help me find a solution. Maybe not just a solution, but a miracle! Your daughter needs you, you need to take care of her until her mother gets better!" the doctor said, comforting.

The professional tried to give him hope, encouraging him to believe that there was a treatment, that his wife would be alright. However, he was certain that there was no chance of recovery.

After a two-hour long wait, Robert was granted permission to see his wife. Seeing her laying in the hospital bed, he fell to his knees and promised her that he would do anything to not lose her.

✠

Seven hours later, the doctor asked him to go home to rest.

Before leaving, he begged the doctor to give him two minutes with his wife. He thanked the professional and entered his wifes' hospital room to say goodbye, not knowing that would be the last time he would get to say it. Caressing her cheeks, he told her to fight for him, because his life did not make sense without her.

Dejected, he exited the room. Walking the hallways of the hospital, he felt as if the walls were getting narrow and started running towards the exit. There he leaned against a wall, lowering himself on his knees. His tears blurred his eyesight.

In the end, he encouraged himself and got in the car, sighing continuously, out of breath. While driving home he could not concentrate. He thought of his wife and what he could do, what solution he could find to prevent a nightmare.

Chapter 2

He arrived home, got out of the car, and walked towards the house, stopping outside the door. Feeling lost, he almost didn't dare to open the door because he knew, his daughter was going to ask where her mother was. Encouraging himself, he reached for the door knob and opened the door. His little girl started running towards him and asked about her mother, what he feared would happen.   Nevertheless, he answered that her mommy was not feeling well and needed to be hospitalized for a couple of days to recover.

"I miss my mommy!" the little girl started crying.

Robert kneeled, taking the child into his arms, trying to comfort her.

Alice, his sister, was in the kitchen preparing dinner, hiding her worry. She went to her brother to ask about the incident. He explained everything that the doctor had told him at the hospital.

She told him to go take a shower while she finishes the dinner. He did so, started the shower, and when looking into the mirror, his eyes were red, his face was scratched, his fingernails were bitten on his right hand.

After getting into the shower, his hair started falling. The skin on his head was stinging when it made contact with the water. He felt numb. Suddenly, he started yelling as loud as he could, wanting to relieve the tension inside of him. His sister and daughter got worried and ran towards Robert to see what had happened. Alice knocked on the bathroom door.

"Brother, are you alright?" she asked, concerned.

"I'm so sorry, I felt the need to let off some steam, I couldn't control myself," he answered, opening the door.

"I understand, but please be careful," Alice pleaded.

She told him to go change and to come down for dinner.

After dinner, Emma felt sleepy. He picked her up and took the little girl to her room, putting her to bed. She asked for a story so she could fall asleep. He read her favorite story about a warrior princess. When the story was done, Emma asked if her mom would get better until tomorrow and if she was coming home. He caressed her cheeks and told his daughter that her mom would indeed get better and come home to them soon enough. He promised her this, but didn't know if he himself believed it.

The next morning, Robert woke up, prepared breakfast for the girl, and headed towards her room to wake her up. He opened the door and walked slowly to her bed.

"Good morning Emma. It's time to wake up, I prepared your favorite breakfast," he shook her slowly, to not startle her.

Emma woke up and they headed downstairs towards the kitchen. There, he poured her milk and chocolate cereal, and she started smiling and hugged him tight and thanked him, expressing how much she loved him. After she ate, Robert took her to school.

On his way back, his sister called. She said that her boss agreed for her to take some time off and she would live with them until his wife got better. He told her he did not want to complicate her life.

"Our parents told us before they died that we need to take care of each other always!" Alice said, almost sobbing.

She then told him that she was going to pick Emma up from school. He thanked her and headed towards the hospital, thinking of his wife and how she felt since he had not heard anything about her since the last time he saw her.

Robert got to the hospital and hurried towards the reception. There, he was asked about his name and who he was visiting, telling them that he was Robert Williams and came to see his wife, Emily Williams. Robert was told to take a seat in the waiting room and that a doctor would come see him soon.

After a short wait, he was greeted by the doctor who was taking care of his wife. He asked about Emily. The doctor said that it would be better to continue the conversation about his wife's well-being in his office. Robert could read on the doctors' face that the situation was not a good one. The professional started telling him about the happenings of last night, when Emily went into a deep coma, and promised that the hospital would do everything they could to bring her back. He also told Robert that his wife suffered from an intracerebral hemorrhage, known as cerebral bleeding. He explained further that this was a sudden bleeding in the brain tissue, inside of the skull, a massive stroke. Emily's chances were low and Robert should be prepared for the worst. The Doctor assured Robert that she would be under supervision at all times and constantly connected to machines.

She was in a persistent vegetative condition, without cognitive neurological functions, not being conscious of the things happening around her.

After hearing the news, Robert felt drained of energy. He did not know how to act anymore. The only thing he knew was that he had to see her immediately and headed to her hospital room. Watching her with immense sadness, kissing her forehead, he told her how much he loved her.

In the evening, the man returned back home, where Alice and his daughter were waiting to hear about Emily's situation.

"Dad, how's mom? When is she coming home?" little Emma asked, as soon as Robert entered the door.

He lied to her and told her that her mother was feeling better but she would not be able to come home soon. She insisted on seeing her mom and Robert said that in a couple of days he would take her to see Emily.

The next morning, Robert told Alice that he had to run some errands and afterwards, would go visit his wife. Robert's sister took the girl to school, but before they left, Emma gave her dad a drawing she made for her mom on which she wrote 'Mom, I want you to get better and to come home to dad and I!' He assured her that he would give it to her mom, hugged her, and promised they would go to the cinema after school. Happily, Emma got into the car, buckled her belt like her mom had taught her, and Alice took her to school, the girl looking back at her father and blowing kisses his way.

After finishing his errands, Robert arrived at the hospital. He parked his car and saw that at the hospital's entrance was a medical team waiting on an ambulance that was approaching at high speed. The doctors took over the victim. Robert was curious and asked a guard what happened, learning that a driver under the influence of alcohol drove into another car. Two people died and the third was seriously injured. He got closer to the ambulance. As he approached, he noticed the doctors were taking the victim into their care. Looking closer, he saw the patient was a child and he felt as if he knew the kid. It was a girl, but he wasn't too sure of who she was because her face was covered by an oxygen mask. He continued to walk towards the entrance and stopped suddenly, turning back and running to the ambulance because he felt something was not right. When he approached the stretcher, the doctors told him he was not allowed to get close to the victim of the accident. Nevertheless, he snuck a look and there she was. The girl laid out on the stretcher, she was his child.

Chapter 3

He was stuporous. Couldn't talk, as if his voice was lost. Everything around him was spinning and the world seemed to be in slow motion. Robert felt as if he was in a nightmare that he could not wake up from.

He started to shout, "She's my child, my daughter Emma. Emma, can you hear me?"

Robert was pushed aside by doctors and called for the guards to identify him. He presented the identity documents and it was confirmed that he was the father, the guards allowing him to enter the hospital immediately.

At the reception, a doctor had announced to him that, sadly, one of the other victims had been his sister, who had passed away on the spot. Robert remained speechless. The doctor also told him that Emma had been taken into the operating room. They asked him to take a seat in the waiting room while he was begging, "Save her, please, I don't want to be alone in this big world, please …," with tears in his eyes.

Robert went to the waiting room and sat down, trembling the whole time, in a state of emotional shock, after the news he had gotten.

There was a mother with her little girl, who was playing in a designated area for children. At one point, the girl approached him with a chocolate bar and asked if he wanted it. Robert looked into the little girl's eyes, affectionately, took the chocolate bar, and thanked her. The little girl told him that if he didn't eat the chocolate, he could give it to his child. Suddenly, Robert burst into tears and scared the little girl. Her mother intervened and explained to the child that the man was upset and it would be best to let him calm down. The little girl's mother asked Robert what had happened, and Robert told her everything. The deeply impressed woman hugged him and told him not to be afraid, to never lose hope. She gave him a phone number and told him her name was Alexandra, she was a scientist, and her daughter's name was Roxy. If he needed help, he should call her. Robert, with a heart full of grief, thanked her gratefully, feeling dumbfounded.

Five hours later, a doctor named Leo, who had taken care of Emma's surgery, came to talk to him. When Robert saw him, he stood up and, in a hurry, walked towards the doctor, asking for an update on how Emma was feeling and what had happened. The doctor patted him on the shoulder and told him to walk outside to the hospital park to calmly discuss the situation of his child. There, they sat on a bench under an oak tree. The doctor explained to him what had happened and discussed Emma's situation.

It was at that moment that Robert found out that Emma had fallen into a deep coma caused by multiple fractures to her spine, skull, and internal bleeding. Upon hearing such terrible news, Robert kneeled down and began to pound the ground with his fists, screaming to the sky.

"Lord, what have I done wrong?" he asked continuously.

Leo tried to calm him down, telling him that everything wasn't gone and there was still hope.

"Please, help me, please!" Robert kept begging.

The doctor assured Robert that he would not give up because, as long as there was hope, there would be a great chance to save them both.

After the tragic news, trying his best to encourage him, he accompanied Robert to the ward where Emma was hospitalized. When he entered the ward, Robert began to tremble, unable to believe that such a disaster had befallen him. Within a few days, he had lost his sister, and the two most important people in his life were in a coma, being kept alive by life support.

Robert asked the doctor if he could stay in the hospital room with his daughter overnight. The doctor on duty approved his request and allowed him to stay with his daughter.

Around midnight, Robert went to see his wife, who was hospitalized in the same unit.

"My dear wife, I have to tell you that Alice has left us and our daughter has suffered a terrible accident. I don't know what to do now. Please, say something, give me a sign!" he pleaded, caressing her face.

Robert looked at her, hoping that she would blink or open her eyes. He watched her for almost 10 minutes, he saw no sign. Robert kissed his wife on the cheek and returned to his daughter.

He sat on the chair next to her bed, held her hand tightly, and fell asleep with his head resting on her bed.

✠

The next day, Robert's best friend, Darius, heard about the tragedy and came to the hospital to support him. When the he saw him, he got up from the chair and hugged him.

"Thank you for coming, Darius. You have always been a good friend and I appreciate your support in moments like these. I still can't believe what happened, but I'm trying to be strong for my family. I'm so lucky to have people like you in my life," Robert said appreciatively, "but Darius, what do I do now?" he asked, after a quick moment of silence.

"Robert, in this big world, I know no man stronger and wiser than you. I am sure you will be able to overcome the difficult situation you are facing right now," Darius comforted him.

After a while, Dr. Leo came back to talk to Robert.

"Go home, take some time. Prepare for your sister's funeral. Please, trust me!" he said to Robert.

He thanked the doctor and left the hospital. His car remained in the hospital parking lot and got into his friend's car. Darius wouldn't let him drive in his current state. On the way, Robert was silent and eventually they arrived home. He opened the door and entered the house, which seemed empty, silent, and sad. He felt alone and lost.

Chapter 4

On Friday the 28th of July 2100, Robert buried his sister. He was exhausted and traumatized.

After he buried his sister, Robert chose to walk home. The sun was almost setting and the moon had started to rise. Robert thought that this was an accurate representation of the ups and downs of human life.

On his way home, Robert was lost in thought. A white car slowly approached him, slowed down, and stopped as he walked on the sidewalk. Two men got out of the car and walked towards him, greeting him. Robert responded to their greeting and asked how he could help them and how they knew him, since he did not know them.

"It's not important that you know us, Robert, what matters is that we know you. We know everything that happens in this city," they explained.

Robert, frightened, told them he would call the police, but one of them said it would be better for him not to do that. Nothing bad would happen to him, they just wanted to talk. Robert agreed to listen to them.

"We discovered that you have two people in a coma who have been admitted to the hospital. We'd like to make you an offer you can't refuse."

Robert tried to take his phone out of his pocket, but one of the men immobilized him and told him they were not playing games. Any wrong move would get him and his family killed. The smart thing to do was to listen to them. They explained the situation to him and then they left, saying they would call him in a few days. Left alone, Robert called Darius and explained what had happened, asking to meet him at his house.

In 2100, corruption and crime were at a very high level. Mafia groups were involved in the sale of human organs all over the world. When it was known that someone was in critical condition, they would try everything they could to persuade the families of the seriously ill to abandon them, to disconnect them from the machines that kept them alive.

When Robert got home and saw Darius waiting for him in front of the house, he felt relieved that he wasn't in this situation alone. Darius noticed the worry on Robert's face and asked him how he was feeling. Robert told him everything that had happened and shared all his fears with him. Darius assured him that he would do everything possible to help him protect his family.

The two men stayed up all night and discussed all possible scenarios that could happen and how to prepare in case of an attack.

The next morning, Darius decided to call a cop friend and tell him about Robert's encounter with the two men and the offer they made. Darius' friend told him that he had heard of such mafia groups, involved in human organ trafficking, and suggested that they should be very careful and to avoid such dangerous people. Darius took the advice seriously and told Robert to be extremely cautious and to not contact these individuals. If Robert was contacted again, he was to inform Darius or his police friend immediately.

✠

Weeks had passed since the tragedy struck Robert. Throughout this time, Robert visited his wife and daughter in the hospital, daily.

Three days had passed since Robert was approached by the two individuals who were part of a mafia group. They had told him that they would call to see what he had decided. It happened exactly as they said. They called him and asked him what decision he had made. Robert answered resolutely that they should leave him alone because he would never give up the most important people in his life and he would do anything in his power to save them.

"Okay, that's your decision, but know that you have made a mistake and there will be consequences, as you will see soon," they threatened Robert, trying to scare him.

Although he was afraid of the consequences, Robert called Darius and his police friend and told them about the call. They arranged to meet.

Before meeting with Darius and his police friend, Robert picked up the phone and called Dr. Leo to explain the situation. The doctor assured him that someone would watch over them at all times and told him to stay calm. They were safe in the hospital and he did not think anything bad would happen. After talking to Dr. Leo, Robert felt a little more at ease.

On the first day he returned to work, at the end of the shift at 7 p.m, he was getting ready to go home, but the company director called him to his office. He told him he was very happy to have him back on the team.

Robert walked home on his usual route. While he wandered, he decided to pass through a park, where he was approached and beaten by some unknown people.

After unexpectedly being beaten and threatened, Robert called Darius. He felt anger and rage like he never had before.

Darius contacted his friend and told him that Robert had been attacked but was alright, with only a few bruises on his face, but nothing that would not heal in a couple of days. The police officer instructed Darius to bring Robert to the police station where he wanted Robert to give a statement.

Arriving at the police station, they entered the officer's office and discussed Roberts' situation. The officer, concerned, told Robert that the human organ mafia had infiltrated the police force due to corruption and they needed to be careful about who they came into contact with.

They came up with a plan for Robert to keep his family safe. The plan was for Robert to contact Dr. Leo and ask him to allow his daughter and wife to be taken out of the hospital, including the life support machines, and to hide them. Robert agreed and asked Darius where he could hide his family from the human organ mafia.
Darius offered a cabin in the mountains of Scotland, given to him by his grandfather. Robert could take his loved ones there to keep them safe.

On the same day, Robert and Darius met with Dr. Leo to persuade him to help them with their plan. When they met, it was evident on Robert's face that he was desperate. He kept asking Leo if Emily and Emma were safe.

Dr. Leo told Robert that he could take his family out of the hospital on his own, but he needed to sign a liability waiver. Leo also offered them breathing apparatus and arranged for transportation in an ambulance.

"Thank you so much, Dr. Leo," said Robert.

While they were grateful for the help, they were also very stressed about Robert's family situation. However, they knew they had to act quickly and deal with it.

Robert signed the liability waiver and then, together with Darius, went to pick up his family from the hospital.

They arrived at their destination after driving for several hours. Darius's cabin in Scotland had a very nicely furnished basement. It had a rough metal door that was hard to break which was perfect for what they needed, a place where Emma and Emily would be safe.

They set up all the machines.

Darius, being an electromechanical engineer, made sure that the life-support machines were functioning properly. After that, he went to buy some surveillance cameras from a nearby town. When he returned with the surveillance cameras, he installed them and made sure they were working perfectly.

Aware that they were in grave danger, they did everything they could to ensure the family's safety, keeping Emily and Emma hidden from any danger. Nobody, except the people Robert trusted, knew where his family was taken..

The next day, Robert received a call from the company's director and was told that he would be able to work from home but would need to come to the company once a month for meetings. Robert was delighted with the understanding that the company had given him. This way, he would not be exposed to external dangers and could continue to carry out his professional activity. It was important for Robert to ensure that he had all the necessary equipment and resources to work efficiently from home and to maintain regular communication with his colleagues and superiors.

Chapter 5

In the following days, everything went just as normal for Robert. Everything had become routine and he had grown accustomed to his situation.

One morning, after several weeks of being hidden with his family in the mountains of Scotland, Leo, the doctor, came to visit and check Emily and Emma's state. After he analyzed the health status of the two, Leo told Robert that there had been no change in their health condition and that he should continue to monitor them. Robert felt a certain disappointment because he had hoped that the health conditions of the two women would significantly improve in the past few weeks. However, he understood the importance of continuous monitoring and was grateful for Leo's advice.

Robert often felt overwhelmed by the responsibility of taking care of his family in this difficult situation. Nevertheless, he tried to remain strong and provide the necessary support to his wife and daughter. Those days he gathered wood, heated and prepared food, and monitored the health status of his family.

After Leo left, Robert went back to the basement where Emily and Emma were being kept.

"My dear wife, the fight does not let me rest," he said, approaching her.

He turned to Emma and kissed her on the cheek.

"I love you, my little girl," he whispered to Emma, watching her intently.

That evening, Robert cooked dinner and sat down at the table. He made risotto, but when he put the first forkful of rice in his mouth, he felt like he had lost his appetite. He tried to eat a second forkful of rice, but he couldn't because he felt devoid of appetite. Robert got up from the table and put the rice in a casserole dish.

Then, he went to sleep. During the night, Robert couldn't sleep at all because he was afraid that someone might break into his house while he slept.

In the morning, when he woke up and had his coffee, he came up with the idea of adopting a dog. Robert thought that a pet would make him feel better.

After he finished his coffee, he began to search online for an animal shelter. He found a local shelter that had several dogs available for adoption. He quickly found an adorable german shepherd dog that he picked up that day and brought home. Robert felt much more at ease knowing he had a furry friend by his side. He named him 'Trust'.

⚔

A few weeks later, following his daily routine, Robert went into the cellar where his loved ones were and noticed something unusual on Emily's body. Her skin appeared to have changed color in some areas. He called Leo and explained what he saw. The doctor told him that sometimes such spots on the skin are normal, but he would need to come and perform a health check.

Later that day, Leo arrived at Robert's and went to check on Emily. After he performed some tests, Leo invited Robert to come out onto the cabin terrace to talk.

Robert made some tea and they went outside, sat on the cabin steps, and began to talk about the test results. Leo found that Emily's condition was getting worse and she would need a stronger treatment. Regrettably, he suggested that Robert prepare for what might happen. After the doctor left, Robert called Darius and asked him to come the next morning.

The next day, Darius arrived at the cabin and suggested Robert to try and rest because he did not look good at all. Robert decided to listen to him and went to his bedroom to rest. After he woke up, he told Darius that he would go into town to buy supplies and asked him to stay with the girls until he returned.

In town, he purchased the supplies and loaded them into his car. Robert decided to go to a pastry shop to buy some cakes. He parked his car

21

in the parking lot and headed towards the pastry shop, which was only a 5-minute walk away. When he arrived at the pastry shop, he bought his favorite cakes, tiramisu and éclairs, and walked back to the parking lot.

On the way back, Robert saw a group of children playing on their phones in front of a building. Then, a great idea came to him. One that Robert didn't know would change his life.

Upon arriving home, Robert was very excited to tell Darius about the idea he had just thought of. When he entered the house, he called out to Darius.

"What happened?" asked Darius.

"I have an idea on how I can save them," Robert explained.

"What idea do you have?" questioned Darius, curious of what Robert had thought about.

They both went into the kitchen and made themselves coffee. After that, Robert began to talk.

"Darius, what if I could create a program or a calculator that could create artificial life or something like an artificial universe?" Robert started to explain what idea had crossed his mind while he watched those kids.

For a few seconds, Darius didn't know whether to take Robert seriously. He thought he was delirious, but still listened to him. Robert started to explain the idea of the program and how he could connect Emily and Emma to himself. Explaining the entire plan, Darius told him that it wouldn't be impossible, but he would have to find a way to connect neurons and memory cells. He would also need to talk to a specialist doctor and a scientist. Robert replied, suggesting that they had Leo as a doctor. Darius agreed, but he said he would still need a scientist. Robert thought for a few seconds and then it came to him.

"I know a lady named Alexandra. I met her in the hospital. I'll contact her," he decided. After all, she had told him to call her if he ever needed any help.

Darius pondered on what Robert said and decided it would be a good idea to present the proposal to Alexandra, so he told Robert to give her a call and see what she had to say about it. Robert immediately called Alexandra and explained his idea to her. She was both amazed and intrigued by their proposition. That type of research would be revolutionary in the scientific field. She agreed to join the project and offer her expertise. They decided to meet the next day. Robert and Darius were very pleased with the positivity Alexandra showed towards their plan.

They then called Leo to tell him about the idea. He was excited about the proposal as well. He was impressed by their enthusiasm and decided to also join the project.

The next day, the four of them worked together on developing the program, bringing new and innovative ideas and discussing how they could implement their research. They didn't hesitate much and each of them started to work on the project and spent many sleepless nights and days doing research and experiments. The group had set up a small laboratory right in the cabin where Robert was hiding and they had everything they needed to create their own program that could attain the idea they had come up with.

Hard work did pay off because they managed to create a device that could be directly connected from the brain and heart to the computer they had invented. The computer worked through a very complex program. The codes in the program were designed to be able to capture real-life memories and implant them into artificial life. Once a person was connected to the computer, they should have felt the same feelings as in real life, without knowing that it was artificial life. Their revolutionary device in hand, Robert was ready to try to connect to the computer created by them.

Initially, he was very worried that it could harm him or have unexpected consequences. Nevertheless, his desire to save his family was stronger than his fear.

Robert's heartbeat was fast. He put the device on his head. Darius connected it to the computer. They did not know what to expect.

"Close your eyes and relax," Darius told him, ready to connect Robert to the computer.

Darius entered the device startup codes.

When Robert was ready, Darius pressed the button to connect the computer to the device installed on Robert. The program started to run. Robert's body shook as if he had an electric shock. Leo monitored him all the time. After his body stopped shaking, Leo said that Robert was still responsive, his heartbeat was normal, and his brain functions were stable. Now they could only wait for a signal on the computer screen they had created, but they couldn't see anything. When the program would write 'Robert is connected', then they would know that their invention was working, but they still had to wait for Robert to return to real life to find out how the artificial life they had created was.

Chapter 6

Everything suddenly lit up in front of Roberts' eyes and he was transported to an amazing artificial world. He felt a strong emotion as everything he saw and felt seemed real.

"We did it!" He cheered, talking to himself.

Nevertheless, he still had doubts because he didn't know if the device connecting the real and artificial lives would work with Emily and Emma.

Robert began to explore the artificial world and found that everything looked and felt the same as in reality. However, there were limits imposed by the codes they created in this artificial universe. They had only created a small map using their codes, but their plan was to expand and develop the artificial universe in the future, just like in reality.

After about six hours of exploring artificial life, Robert decided to return to the real world. Before he did that, he wanted to see his house in the artificial world. In order to do that, had to enter the exact code and data that would take him to the house. He was immediately teleported there and was very excited to go inside. When he entered the house, it was empty. He went to his bedroom and lay down.

"Disconnect me," he said, ready to return to his team.

The program received the command and sent a signal to the computer in the real world. Then, a message appeared on the computer screen saying 'Disconnecting'. Darius saw the message and pressed the button that allowed Robert to return to the real world.

Back in the real world, he saw Darius, Alexandra, and Leo in a fog. His vision was blurry, but when he regained his senses, after a few minutes, Robert started crying tears of joy with his friends.

During the following days, they corrected certain errors in the program and improved artificial life.

They then made the decision to try and connect Emma and Emily to artificial life. The four of them began to install and connect the devices between the two girls to the computer they called the ALU (Artificial Life Universe) device. After they prepared them and made sure everything worked properly, Robert also connected himself.

Darius began to input the connection codes and transfer all the memory data. They were not sure if it would work for Emma and Emily, as they were in a very aggravated condition. However, they decided to risk it and connect them.

Darius entered the last code into the program and the transfer was made. Now they just had to wait and after a few minutes, a message appeared on the computer screen indicating that the data transfer was complete and that it was connected to ALU.

"Now we will wait and see," Darius said, looking at Alexandra and Leo.

Meanwhile, Robert woke up in ALU, on a field somewhere far from his home because the program had decided to transfer him there. The program had created a bad fog, barely visible at a distance of five meters.

Robert ran towards his house, full of excitement. He still did not know if the transfer was successful. As he approached his house in a hurry, two shadows began to appear in the distance. He hoped it was not a program error or a figment of his memory.

"Emily! Emily! Emily!" he started shouting.

Robert approached the shadows he saw. The fog evaporated and revealed Emily and Emma. He burst into tears of joy, and Emily, confused and unaware that she was in an artificial place, looked at him as if he was crazy.

"My love, why are you crying?" she asked, approaching him.

"Oh, I have so much to tell you!" Robert babbled. It was insane and he still couldn't believe they had been successful in creating this world.

Emily looked at him confused while Robert took Emma in his arms, saying,"I can't believe it, we did it".

Robert was so grateful that, in the end, after so much time he had to wait and the effort he and his team put into this project, he managed to meet his family in ALU.

The three of them entered the house. Emily asked him why he was so emotional and Robert, still having tears in his eyes, said,"I'll tell you after dinner, my dear".

Robert and Emily began to prepare dinner. It was so amazing but so odd, because it had been months since he had dinner with his family. He knew that it wasn't real, but he accepted it. It didn't matter to him whether he was in reality or in artificial life, what was important was that he was with his family.

After dinner, Emma went to the living room to watch cartoons. Emily and Robert stayed in the kitchen to clean up. At one point, Emily hugged Robert and started asking him questions regarding his reaction from earlier.

"Now, can you tell me why you cried and said those things before we entered the house?" she questioned.

Robert was silent for a few seconds.

"Let's sit down," he said, taking her hands in his.

He began to explain the whole story and revealed that the house they were in was not real, but a copy created by a program in a computer and that they were actually connected to a device that linked real life to artificial life. Emily was in shock because she didn't understand how this was possible.

"What do you mean? Where did you come up with these ideas? What happened to Emma? Why are you telling me that Alice is dead? I was just at her place yesterday," Emily asked. She had so many questions and didn't know which one she wanted answered first..

Robert looked into her eyes.

"These are memories that the codes chose, in fact. This was a day before you got sick and fell into a coma. All three of us went to Alice's, but unfortunately, what I'm telling you now is true. Believe me," he sighed, realizing how difficult explaining the situation was.

Emily was stunned and confused by what Robert had just said. She remembered being at Alice's and couldn't understand how it could all be an illusion.

Robert began to explain how everything worked, that there was an artificial world created by a program, which was connected to real life through a connecting device. In this world, they had experiences similar to those in real life, but everything was created and controlled by codes and algorithms.

Robert asked Emily to go with him in the car to the city to show her, because Darius hadn't yet introduced any character or person from reality in the real world. They took Emma and the three of them got into their car and drove to the city. There were no other cars on the road. Robert looked at Emily, who was in shock. As they approached the city center, they parked the car and got out. The place was completely empty, with no sign of human life. Emily kept saying that it's not possible, still perplexed. After she saw that what Robert had said was true, they went back home. The whole way back, Emily was lost in thought and silent.

Back home, Robert went to the bathroom to prepare the bathtub with water for the little one. After giving her a bath, he took her to her bedroom.

"Daddy, why was there no one in the city and why were all the shops closed?" Emman asked, her face expressing confusion.

Robert replied that it was late, so no one was on the streets.

He put Emma to sleep and went to the kitchen.

Emily was sitting at the table. She had made herself a coffee and her stare was fixated on the kitchen TV.

"Emily, are you okay?" Robert asked her, nervous about the entire situation.

"Are the TV programs fake too?" she asked, still not looking at him.

"Yes," Robert said, "because they are created by algorithms and programs installed in the computer."

"So we are, kind of, like game characters," Emily thought out loud.

"No," Robert said, "no one can control you, only you can control yourself. My dear, our only chance to be together is here, in this universe."

"Universe?" Emily asked.

"Yes, universe," he replied, "our plan is to improve the artificial world just like in reality, and it's possible, but I need your help. Emily, my love, in the real world, the doctors told me that we have no chance, and you know that I don't want to be without you and our daughter."

Despite all this, Emily began to cry. Then, Robert took her in his arms and kissed her. As he held her face, he looked into her eyes, saying, "It will be okay. You won't realize that this world is fake. I guarantee it, I promise."

Emily nodded in agreement, but she wondered what would happen to Emma.

"We won't tell her. Even if we do tell her, she won't understand the situation, but we'll explain it to her when the time is right. Tomorrow morning, when you wake up, I won't be here anymore, but I'll connect all the time, especially in the evening, so that Emma will understand that I'm leaving for work in the morning and coming back home in the evening," explained Robert.

Emily asked him not to leave her alone.

"I will never leave you, my dear, but for now, I can't stay here because I have to find a solution to transfer you both to this world without being connected in real mode. I sense that we are close to succeeding," Robert continued.

Emily began to realize that everything Robert said made sense. She trusted that he would succeed with his plans.

Following their conversation, they went to Emma's bedroom to be together. Robert held Emily in his arms, and at one point, she fell asleep. Robert kissed her forehead and willed her to be strong and to never forget how loved both her and their daughter was.

Then, Robert said the word 'disconnect me' and the program transferred him back to reality.

Chapter 7

When Robert woke up, he sat up on the edge of the bed. Darius, Alexandra, and Leo asked him how he felt. Robert smiled at them and gushed, "I've seen them! The device works!"

Robert was very happy. He still could not believe they succeeded.

Leo was wondering what the next steps were and Darius replied, explaining, "We need to make sure Robert connects every evening. Today I'll start updating the program properly."

In the following days, Robert created a routine.

Every evening he connected to the ALU device to meet with his family.

Darius had moved in with him because he worked online as well and could stay with Robert.

Alexandra and Leo came three times a week to work on their ideas to improve the program.

After a few weeks, Leo performed tests on Emily and Emma and found that their health had deteriorated significantly and Robert decided to connect to the ALU device and talk to Emily about her situation. During their conversation, some anomalies occurred. Robert noticed that she would repeat her words.

Immediately, he returned to the real world to talk to his friends about the anomaly. The four of them realized that they needed an immediate solution, so they began to list all the plans and ideas they had. They concluded that they needed to find a way to connect Emily and Emma to the ALU without being connected through the device. They also needed to find a way to transfer cells and neurons, memory cells included and to begin to work on their project, taking into account all the implications and risks.

After some time of studying, they found a way, and Robert came up with an idea to create a nanorobot that could be introduced into the human brain and record all memory data and recreate them in VR. The four began looking for specialists to produce the nanorobot. The next day, they found a company in Japan that dealt with such projects and sent them an email with their plan.

Meanwhile, they continued to work on their project, considering all implications and risks.

A few days later, they received a response from the Japanese company and they agreed to meet. They had a series of meetings with experts in the fields of neuroscience, engineering, and ethics to discuss their project in more detail and evaluate the risks associated with the introduction of nanorobots into the human brain. In the end, they decided to proceed with the project with extreme caution and they signed strict confidentiality agreements with the Japanese company.

They developed and tested the nanorobots for months, so they could make sure that it would be safe to record memory data and recreate it in ALU. Eventually, they concluded that their nanorobots were ready to be tested on a human subject.

Robert reconnected to ALU to discuss their progress with Emily. She was very excited and tried to encourage Robert, telling him that he had nothing to lose. However, as a mother, she would want to be the first to be tested, not Emma, in case something was wrong. Robert kissed her and thanked her for her support.

"Robert, I want you to know that what you've created here is amazing. Artificial life has taken on a special aspect. I don't even feel like I'm in a fake place," Emily said to him, proud of what her husband had achieved.

Robert smiled at her and disconnected.

⚓

In the following days, the Japanese genetics engineers, who had left for a while, returned to Scotland and Darius picked them up from Glasgow airport and brought them to the cabin where they were hiding.

Robert welcomed them properly, made them coffee and tea, and then they began to discuss their plan. They decided to start the test the next day.

The Japanese engineers woke up early the next day and started to prepare the introduction of the nanobots into Emily's brain. When Robert saw them, he was surprised by how organized they were. The robotic engineers inflated a hermetically sealed room like a balloon, where they would introduce the nanorobots. They brought Emily into the hermetically sealed room and prepared her for implantation.

Doctor Leo and the robotic engineers were dressed in special suits, while Robert waited outside the hermetically sealed room with Alexandra and Darius. It was an important day for them.

The cell engineers specialists and the doctor began the implantation procedure. It was not a complicated procedure, but the effects it could produce were unknown. The nanorobots would be implanted with a device similar to a syringe.

Leo started the procedure and implanted the nanorobots. After that, they analyzed Emily's situation and everything seemed stable. They had to wait for the nanorobots to do the job. The whole procedure took twenty-eight hours. After the nanorobots copied all the necessary data to create a kind of artificial brain, which would not be real, it scanned the cerebellum, all the cells and neurons, and then recreated them as codes.

Emily was transferred to a special bed in an adjacent room following the completion of the procedure. Doctor Leo and the cell engineers specialists began to analyze the data collected by the nanorobots and decoding it to create a virtual version of her brain. The task took days to complete, but eventually, they successfully generated the artificial brain.

Robert, Alexandra, and Darius waited anxiously. They were worried about Emily and wondered if everything would work. After they finished the process, Doctor Leo invited everyone to the lab he had created in the house to present the results. In the center of the room was a hologram of Emily's artificial brain, projected in the air. It was amazing to see how nanotechnology could create such a complex and detailed replica of the human brain.

They now had an exact virtual copy of Emily's brain and they could try to connect it to a computer and attempt to interact with it. Doctor Leo and the Japanese genetics engineers began to further develop the technology and tried to perfect it. Robert, Alexandra, and Darius closely followed them.

Robert would have to make the decision to disconnect Emily from the life support machines. That day had arrived.

The team of Japanese genetic engineers, together with Robert's team, were prepared to take a big step in science and robotics.

They created a device called an artificial brain (AB). The device was the size of a mobile phone and was attached to Emily's skull. Very small tubes emerged from it, and at the end of them were needles through which nanorobots returned to the AB device. After that, the device was attached and directly connected to the intelligent ALU computer.

Robert connected to the ALU device to talk and prepare Emily. He would stay with Emma and tell her that her mother was going to the store.

Robert was transferred to the artificial world to meet his wife.

"My love, are we ready to take this risky but deserved step?" Robert asked Emily anxiously.

"I'm ready, yes. Whatever happens, happens," she answered.

She made Robert promise not to give up, no matter what happened.

Afterwards, Robert took the little one and went to the park to play. There, Emma went to the swings and Robert sat on a bench and watched over her.

Meanwhile, in the real world, genetic, robotics experts, and Robert's team began the data transfer operation from the nanorobots that were connected and implanted in a special computer made for this operation.

The nanorobots were made of a very durable material and there were no risks of them being easily destroyed, rusted, or affecting the ALU program in any way.

As the data transfer operation began, the team noticed that the data flow was much faster than expected, which led to slight panic. However, after they analyzed the data, they discovered that the transfer had been successful and without problems.

Back in the artificial world, Emily had laid down and closed her eyes and then her body had been completely erased from the artificial world.

The installed algorithms and programs had started to function and had to erase all the data that was already installed, to make room for the codes and data copied by the nanorobots.

In the real world, the computer had signaled the reconstruction of the artificial body in ALU.

After some time, ALU recreated Emily in the initial state she was in before being erased from the artificial world. This time however, all her memories and consciousness were fully transferred to ALU. Emily woke up and opened her eyes, then quickly got up. She knew that before she disappeared, she was in an artificial world, but she wasn't sure if she had returned to the same world. She was very scared that all of Robert's and those involved work had not worked and so she quickly left the house and ran to the park, where Robert was with their daughter. When she saw Robert, she shouted for him. Robert saw her and shouted her name back.

"Do you think it worked?" she asked, scared of what might have happened.

"I'm going back to the real world to see, but know that we have one more step to take, which is to disconnect your physical body from ALU. Then I'll come back here to see if it worked," Robert let her know.

"I love you so much," Emily professed.

At the end of the day, after putting the little one to sleep, Robert returned to reality.As he got there, he told the rest that it was time to disconnect Emily.

"Do you want to do this yourself?" Darius asked, wanting to give Robert this one moment of silence with the physical body of his wife.

"Yes, I would appreciate it a lot," confessed Robert.

Everyone cleared the room to give him some space.

Robert approached Emily's body and began to remove the device that connected her to the ALU. After that, Robert stroked her forehead, saying, "I hope it works, my dear."

Emily's body would still be connected to life support machines, only as a precaution.

The whole team involved in the project was in a very emotional state because they were all eagerly waiting for the outcome of Robert's project.

After the ALU device was disconnected from Emily, Robert had to return to the artificial world to see if everything worked as he expected. He sat back on the bed and Darius reinstalled the device that connected him to the ALU.

Alexandra, Leo, and Darius approached him. They all leaned in and hugged Robert.

"We are with you until the end," they told him.

Robert was transferred to the artificial world.

Chapter 8

Arriving back in the artificial world, Roberts' heartbeat was racing as he was filled with emotions.

ALU had teleported Robert right in front of his house. He entered and began to look for Emily and Emma. Robert could not find them at all and began to worry but, after a while, he heard a melody coming from the house's attic. He climbed the ladder that went up to the attic, reaching the entrance. Sticking his head in, suddenly his worry disappeared because Emily was there with Emma.

"Emma, come to Daddy!" he shouted, excited to see her again.

The little girl ran to him and he picked her up into a hug. Emily went and hugged him too, exclaiming, "I had no doubt that you wouldn't succeed,"

He kissed her and said, "I love you."

All three went down to the living room. There, Emily asked Robert what would happen next and they talked about the next steps until night had fallen.

At the end of the day, Robert returned to the real world. There, when he woke up, Darius and everyone involved asked him if everything went according to plan.

"Yes, and I couldn't have done it without your help and involvement. Thank you very much and I love you all so much," Robert answered with a smile on his face.

The group hugged him and began to cry tears of joy. They had finally succeeded in completing their mission to create the wonderful artificial world called ALU.

Robert was very grateful for all the work and effort put in by the team of Japanese researchers, developers, and engineers who helped him fulfill the mission he had created.

The next day, Robert was asked by the specialists who were assisting him if he was ready to take the next step with little Emma. Robert replied that he was ready.

The specialists began preparing her, following the same procedure as they did with Emily, after the nanorobots were introduced and the substrate in the little one's brain was prepared, and then connected to the ALU. Robert was much more confident in this installation process because it had worked with his wife before. Joined by the team assisting him, he disconnected Emma from the ALU, and now he would return to the artificial world to confirm that the transition was complete. Robert was very nervous when he arrived in the ALU.

Upon arriving home, Emily was in front of their house, washing the windows. Robert asked her where Emma was, Emily letting him know that she saw Emma play in the garden. He let out a sigh of relief and asked, "Thank God you gave me the strength to succeed. How is she? Did she look disturbed in any way?"

Emily said that she did not. The girl's version in the artificial world would always appear in her bed and so, the little girl thought she was sleeping, since she did not know they were living in this ALU.

Robert went to his daughter and took her in his arms. He was very happy and proud of his family. After spending some time with his daughter, he went to Emily and asked for her opinion on what she thought they should do with their bodies in the real world. Robert was beyond excited that he created an amazing artificial world but still, he didn't accept to lose them from the real world. Emily told him that any sacrifice will have a gain and that no matter what decision he made, she would always support him. Robert thanked her with a smile on his face.

As usual, at the end of the evening, Robert returned to the real world.

When he woke up, there was a lot of commotion and he was very confused, not knowing what had happened. Darius approached him and said, "Emma woke up from her coma."

Robert went into shock and exclaimed, "How is that possible?" looking at Leo, the doctor in the team.

Leo hastily explained that there were certain situations where the treatment was successful and coma patients woke up. Emma's situation was serious and she would have to go to the emergency room. The doctor called a helicopter to come and pick Emma up. Robert approached the little girl and began to cry when he saw her with her eyes open. Emma tried to say something, but she was exhausted.

"Everything is okay, my little girl. You are with your daddy now," he comforted her.

When the helicopter arrived, they immediately transported the little girl on board. Doctor Leo requested that Emma be admitted to the city where he worked, in Glasgow. He boarded the helicopter as well, and they flew to the hospital. Robert and Darius got in the car and headed the same way. Alexandra remained with the Japanese specialists to ensure things would not go wrong with the machines at home.

After a few hours of driving, they arrived at the hospital where Emma was cared for. They went to the reception and identified themselves, Robert as the father of the little girl who was brought in by helicopter and Darius as a family friend. The hospital receptionist asked them to stay in the waiting room until a doctor came to see them.

Shortly, they were greeted by Doctor Leo, who informed them that Emma had been put in the intensive care unit and they would have to wait until they would be able to visit her.

A few hours of waiting later, Doctor Leo came to inform them that Emma's condition was stable, but she needed urgent surgery to remove some blood clots in her brain. Robert asked when the operation would take place and Dr. Leo informed him that it would take place the following morning.

"I will make sure she's alright, don't worry. Go and rent a hotel and then you can come and visit her before the surgery," he comforted Robert.

That's what they did. Prior to the surgical procedure, Robert came with Darius to visit the girl. Their doctor greeted them and invited them to enter the room where the girl was admitted and also informed them that he would be assisting the surgery, along with other specialist surgeons.

Robert and Darius entered the room and saw the girl lying in bed, waiting to enter operation. They were overwhelmed with emotion and concern while they stood by her bed. The two men stayed with Emma, until the doctor told them she needed rest before the procedure, and advised them to do the same.

The following morning, Robert and Darius met with Dr. Leo at the hospital. Together with other specialist surgeons, they prepared the operating room. Robert and Darius stood in a corner of the operating room, carefully observing each movement of the doctors. The operation lasted several hours and all the medical staff and specialists put all their expertise and skills into saving the little girl's life. Eventually, the surgery was successful, and the girl was taken to the recovery room. When Emma woke up from the anesthesia, a nurse called Robert to the room. He was trembling with joy. He approached the bed, leaning over and gently hugging her.

"Daddy's here," Robert said, while he caressed her face gently.

Robert told her that she was in the hospital because she had an accident and that now she needed to rest and stay calm. Emma asked where mommy was and he replied that her mom was somewhere else and would come soon to see her. Robert did not feel good about lying to his daughter, but she calmed down and fell asleep. She was exhausted and tired.

At one point, Doctor Leo came to visit Emma in the ward and asked Robert to step outside with him. The two of them got some coffee and went to the park, where they sat on a bench.

Leo explained to Robert that there was one more step to take. The girl would need to have spinal surgery and then enter a recovery program.

✠

On the third day, Emma was feeling better.

Robert returned to the ward and decided to tell her the truth about her mother. He explained that Emily had fallen into a coma and the doctors did not know if she would recover. Emma listened to her father, breathless, and burst into tears, afraid for her mommy. Robert picked her up and tried to calm her down. He told her how much her mother loved her, how much they both did. Eventually, Emma slowly started to grasp the situation her mother was in, expressing how terrified she was.

"My little angel, you don't have to be afraid. Daddy will be with you all the time and will protect you. Please, understand that no matter what happens to Mommy, I will always be here for you. Your mother wouldn't want us to be helpless and not have each other," exclaimed Robert.

He kissed her forehead and said, "Now try to rest, Daddy's little angel."

Robert left the ward and ran into Leo in the hallway. The doctor stopped him and asked how he was feeling.

"I'm fine, thank you very much," replied Robert, trying to offer a smile.

Then Robert asked about Emily and whether she would recover. Leo was very worried about Emily's health.

"It's been months since your wife has been in a coma and her condition has worsened. There's a big difference between Emily's situation and Emma's situation. I'm sorry, Robert. If you want to keep Emily on life support, you can, but know that her situation is critical," Leo informed him, worry showing on his face.

"I understand. I just want to tell you, my family and I appreciate your support," Robert said, feeling an immense amount of gratitude for the doctor.

After that, Robert went to the hotel where he was staying and met Darius. He told his friend that he would go to Scotland and asked him if he should tell Emily that their daughter had recovered.

"It depends on you and how you feel. I'll support you in whatever decision you make," Darius replied.

Robert asked him if he could go to the hospital instead of him to see the little one.

"Of course," his friend replied. He would do anything to help Robert.

The next morning, Robert left for the house where he was taking refuge in the Scottish mountains.

There, he reconnected to the ALU device with the help of Alexandra and went to meet Emily. He was very happy, eager to tell her what had happened. His wife asked him why he hadn't reconnected, as she hadn't seen him for five days and Emma had asked where daddy was. She had to tell her that he had gone on a business trip for a few weeks. Then, Robert realized that if he told her the truth that Emma had recovered, it might affect Emily, knowing that she was connected to the artificial world and that her daughter from that world was false.

So, Robert decided not to tell her the truth. Not to demoralize Emily. He lied to her that he had something important to do and couldn't reconnect to the ALU, but he promised her that he would try not to let it happen again. Robert explained that he would have to leave for London to meet some colleagues for work, and he would have to work on a project for his company. She understood and said, "No problem, but let's have dinner together."

"Of course," he replied, happily.

After dinner, Robert took the little one to her room as usual.

"Daddy, I love you," she said to him sweetly.

"I love you too, my little angel," he replied, hugging her.

Emma fell asleep and Robert went downstairs to the living room to talk to Emily about what would happen to their bodies in reality.

Robert explained that they would have to be disconnected from the respirators and that they would have to be buried, leaving aside the truth about Emma. Emily understood and told Robert to not be emotional. They would no longer be in the real world; however, they would be here all the time. This was now the reality for them.

Emily kissed Robert and told him how much she loved him. Robert, thoughtful but also happy at the same time, disconnected and he was transferred back to the real world.

Returned to the real world, Alexandra asked him what would happen now, and Robert said he would call the Japanese genetic engineering specialists and tell them that their work had been successfully completed and that they could now return to Japan.

He picked up the phone and called them, thanking them immensely and saying that without their help, he wouldn't have been able to bring his project to life. The Japanese told him that he was a strong man, that it had been their pleasure to work with him, and that if he ever needed them in the future, he shouldn't hesitate to contact them. Robert also told them that he would transfer the money the next morning, but they replied, "Don't worry, we don't need money. It was a unique experience and we learned new technology and nanorobotics techniques with your help. Thank you."

After that, Robert thanked Alexandra for staying to watch over Emily and the ALU computer.

The next morning, Robert left for London.

Arriving at the hospital Emma was in, he met Darius and Leo for a coffee. Robert started a conversation about his daughter and wife's situation. Leo informed him that in a few days, Emma would have spinal surgery, but he assured Robert that she would be fine. She was very strong and would recover quickly.

As for Emily, Leo regretfully suggested to Robert that it was time to disconnect her from the ventilators, but the decision was his.

And after all this, on the next day, after the spine surgery his daughter had, Robert made the decision to disconnect Emily from the respiratory machines.

Before leaving for Scotland, Robert went to the hospital to see his little girl again, telling her that he had to leave for Scotland to take care of something, but a lady named Alexandra would come and take care of her. This lady had a daughter and Emma could talk to her or watch TV together and keep her company.

Robert, Darius, and Leo left for Scotland.

Upon arriving in Scotland, Alexandra was ready to leave for London to stay with Emma. She talked to her husband to bring their daughter to the hospital where Emma was admitted, to introduce her to the girl.

After Alexandra left, Robert and the other two entered the basement where Emily was connected to the respiratory machines. Robert approached Emily, looking at her. It was clear that her condition was critical. Sighing, he told Leo that it was time. Leo started preparing to disconnect the body from the respiratory machines.

Robert went outside, leaving Darius and Leo to take care of disconnecting Emily. There, he took out his phone and called a funeral home company. With the help of the funeral staff, they made plans and set a date for the funeral. The staff asked Robert to contact them when he was ready for them to come, but he replied that they could come today. He explained why, they understood, and they would wait for Robert to call them to prepare Emily for the funeral.

After the phone call, Robert went back inside and returned to the basement.

There, Leo and Darius were looking at him worried.

"It's done," informed Leo.

Robert, with tears in his eyes, said, "She is no longer here with us, but she is still alive in the artificial world and that is what is important to me."

Robert informed his friends that he had talked to the funeral company.

After a few minutes, he sent a message to the people who would handle the funeral to come. Robert also decided that his wife would be cremated.

Three days later, the day came when Robert would say goodbye to his wife in the real world. Following the cremation, Robert took the ashes and returned to the cabin where they stayed. There, he placed the urn with ashes above the fireplace and placed a photo of his wife next to it. His plan was that, when the little one recovered, he would take her with him and they would pour the ashes into a river.

On that evening, Robert reconnected to the ALU device and met with his wife and daughter, whom he embraced as usual. Although he knew that his wife in the artificial world was fake, he didn't feel any difference.

Later, Robert secretly told his virtual wife that her funeral had taken place that day. He couldn't hold back the tears while he told her. Emily encouraged him, telling him that she was proud of him.

After spending some time there, Robert returned to the real world. Darius asked him what would happen next, and Robert told him that after Emma got better, they would move back home to Cambridge.

The next day, Robert and his friends connected the ALU computer to a battery-powered accumulator so they could transport it by car. He decided to bring the computer with him to London so he could connect to it daily and meet Emily in the artificial world.

When they arrived at the hotel in London, Robert and Darius installed the ALU device and prepared it for continuous use. The intelligent computer was connected to a power source and was never to be turned off.

One afternoon, Robert went to see his daughter, who was still in the hospital. Emma looked much better and was recovering very quickly.

He told Emma that her mother was no longer with them and had passed away. The news hit the little girl very hard. She began to cry and accused Robert of lying. He tried to calm her down and explained that he hadn't lied and that it was better for her mother not to suffer.

Together, they looked through a photo album and shared memories of Emily. Robert gave the little girl a necklace with a locket containing her mother's photograph and told her she would always have her mother with her.

He visited his daughter every day at the hospital until Dr. Leo informed him that she could go home in two days but would need to do some recovery therapy.

After talking to Leo, Robert called Darius and announced him that they could take the little girl home.

Before discharging his daughter, Robert took all the equipment and technology used, including the ALU device, to his home in Cambridge. He then returned to London that same evening.

The next morning, Leo called Robert and let him know that Emma was ready to go home immediately. Robert went to the hospital to pick up his little girl and found her dressed up in a beautiful blue dress like the sea. When she saw him, Emma smiled and said, "Daddy, I'm ready to go home." In a few moments, Robert sat Emma in a wheelchair, and they left for the house. Meanwhile, in the hospital corridor, nurses and doctors applauded Robert. He felt emotional and excited. Suddenly, Leo hugged him and said, "Well done Robert, well done!" and told him to expect a visit soon.

Robert and Emma arrived home in Cambridge after their journey.

As he entered the house with his little girl, Robert had a strange feeling. He did not know why he felt so sad. Although he had succeeded in saving both his wife and daughter, his plans had been changed by God's will, and now Emma was his sole responsibility. He was in a delicate situation, with his wife deceased but with Emma in his life. He had to get used to this situation and provide the best education for his daughter.

Robert transformed his office into a sort of scientific laboratory, where he installed the ALU technology. From now on, he only connected to the ALU computer when Emma was not there, to protect her from knowledge of this technology and the fact that her mother had been re-made in an artificial world. Robert always made sure the office was closed and told Emma that important things related to his profession were there, so she never went inside.

In the following months, Emma underwent the necessary treatment and did rehabilitation exercises, gradually healing each day.

Chapter 9

Robert's life in the last year had been extraordinarily tough, but he managed to overcome every obstacle that came his way.

It had been a year since Robert lost his sister, his wife was recreated in an artificial world, and his daughter recovered from a deep coma after several months. He was a strong man, hard to break, and for him, every day was an adventure. Recently, Robert had been working on the technology he created a year ago, developing the technology called ALU. The artificial world looked exactly like the real one and there was no visible difference. People who were connected through the specially created device or people who transferred their entire consciousness through the AB (artificial brain) device lived just like in reality.

The ALU system was designed to replicate everything in reality. For example, if a person suffered a fracture or a cut, they would feel the pain but would heal very quickly. The advantage of the artificial world was that there would be no serious illnesses and the lifespan of 100 years would not apply there. In that world, a person would connect and live an infinite life as long as the ALU computer was connected to a power source.

One day, Robert was coming back from work, and, on his way home, he was thinking about how he would be able to have a better income to afford the improvement of the ALU project and to offer a better life to his daughter. On his way home, he picked Emma up from school, and took her home.

When he arrived at home, Robert called his best friends, Darius, Leo, and Alexandra, to come to his house to discuss a plan he had in mind. The three agreed to meet in three days, on Sunday, at Robert's house.

On the day of the meeting, Robert prepared a barbecue for his friends while Emma was playing with Alexandra's daughter, Roxi.

After some time, Robert, Alexandra, Leo, and Darius sat around the barbecue, and Robert presented his plan. The idea was to use the ALU device to offer other people the chance to use it, perceived through an entrance fee to the artificial universe. Darius asked what the value of this fee would be, and Robert explained that it would depend on the client's requirements. For example, a person who would only want access to a small house and a car, but with certain system access restrictions, would have a lower fee. In the artificial world, the person could gradually grow, but they would have to meet the same conditions as in the real world, which meant going to work and doing projects to improve their financial situation. Another option would be for a millionaire who would want to have an estimated wealth of five million pounds to pay a fee, both in the real world and in the artificial world. The advantage of the millionaire would be that they could grow as a very fast businessman because they could make investments and have access to valuable business information in the artificial world.

"Imagine that now you can connect to this device and practice any operation or tests that you cannot do in the real world. Anyone can experience things in the artificial world and then apply them in the real world. My idea is to turn ALU into a single universe. Meaning that, there will only be one main computer with infinite memory, located in a specially designed place. Each buyer of the ALU device will have their own device and their own ALU computer, but with limits. However, they will be able to access the main computer through a connection and another device that will be incorporated into ALU. I named this other device the luminous radio shock source (IRSS). This device will be able to emit radio pulses like an extremely fast blink of an eye, and the pulse wave can cover an extraordinarily long distance. This source is extraordinary because it is a combination of a light source and a transmission radio source and does not require such a connection," explained Robert excitedly.

Darius asked him what would happen if IRSS lost its signal. Robert replied, "If IRSS loses its signal, there will be no problem in my calculations. Let's assume that in the event that the connection is interrupted, then the person who, for example, is visiting in another ALU system, will be instantly transferred back to their ALU system."

"So, everything should be ok?" Darius asked, still not sure of the idea.

"Yes. We will allocate each computer in a certain way, like a planet with certain places that can be accessed imaginatively. The central ALU is a sun or the center of the galaxy, and the other ALU devices and systems are planets, but they all orbit around the sun or the center of the galaxy. Our device will be the same. It will all depend on a single artificial universe that will be ALU. Additionally, I want to mention that each ALU computer and device will be connected to the ALU central through a kind of artificial tunnel, with an extraordinarily powerful energy, almost like teleportation. Don't forget that with this device, we will be able to create codes that will generate certain things, including objects such as the portal. It will also be connected with the help of the attached IRSS device, which will allow you to move from one system to another, only if you have access from another ALU system. For example, if your brother also has an ALU computer, we will be able to create a kind of interconnected virtual computer network, which will allow users to connect and interact with other ALU systems in the network," explained Robert further.

Darius, Alexandra, and Leo understood Robert's idea, but Alexandra asked why there would be differences between the poor and the rich. Robert replied that the difference lies in the fact that some wealthy individuals would always be ignorant and continuously desire to be above the middle class. He believed that the idea could be exploited to generate money through taxes and to modernize the corporation and the ALU universe. Additionally, he mentioned that wealthy people should not be able to harm others. Robert emphasized that he was prepared to answer any questions regarding the ALU program and any possibilities that may arise during its development.

After a few days, Robert invited his friends again to come and work on the project, and they gathered at his house.

Robert invited them into his office and laid out some papers on the table, which contained sketches and plans for the promotion and development of their project. He began to explain each step that needed to be followed and the priorities that needed to be completed in order to finish the project. The second time around, it would be necessary to have a space where they could carry out their work and then find a way to promote the project.

After Robert finished his explanation, he asked, "Do you know anyone or anywhere we could build a laboratory?"

Alexandra interrupted Robert and said, "My husband has a warehouse on the outskirts of the city that is not being used. It has electricity and water, but it needs some minor renovations."

She then mentioned to Robert that they should leave the promotion to Leo because he knew a television station that could help. Leo's plan was to make an appearance on a science and technology show. There, Robert could present their project.

The four of them didn't hesitate for long and got to work in the following days and weeks. In the end, they managed to move all the technology and to install it properly. The group set up surveillance cameras, the doors of the warehouse were heavily constructed to resist break-ins, and the windows had steel bars and metal shutters. The warehouse looked very secure, and in case of a power outage, they had backup generators that would immediately kick in. Thus, they would have no issues with the ALU system. Robert was thrilled with what they had accomplished together, in only one day.

After a few months, during which they moved the ALU technology and set up their laboratory, the day came when Leo received a call from his friend who worked for a television station called BBC Technology.

Robert asked Darius when the show would take place. Darius called Robert back and informed him that the show would be in one week, on Friday. He was delighted with the news from Darius and told his colleagues that it was time to prepare, to ensure they would have an outstanding presentation on that day.

Every day, Robert and his colleagues rehearsed, and finally, Friday arrived. They created another special ALU computer for this show, and Alexandra took Emma to her sister's place to take care of her until Robert returned home, around 4:00 PM.

Robert, Alexandra, Leo, and Darius set off for London to reach the BBC Technology show, which started at 8:00 PM. The four arrived there 45 minutes early. They were offered coffee, and the show's team began to prepare them.

At 8:00 PM, the show began. As usual, the show host introduced the group, which, by now, had become the bestest of friends. During the show, Robert and his friends explained how the ALU technology worked and the benefits it could bring. They did, however, not mention anything about Emily, because Robert didn't want anything to be accidentally revealed. After Robert explained everything about the device, the show host asked if they could do a demonstration. Robert answered affirmatively and asked the show host if he would like to connect to the ALU device together. Once the ALU device was ready for connection, Darius asked the show host if he was ready to experience an unforgettable moment. The man responded positively, and Darius entered the connection data into the ALU computer. Robert and the elderly man sat on two chairs. Darius, with the help of the ALU device, placed a kind of special helmet on their heads, through which they could connect to the computer. Darius told them to close their eyes and relax.

At that moment, the BBC Technology show had an audience of 15 million viewers.

After Darius asked them to close their eyes, he pressed the button on the computer keyboard, which initiated the data transfer between the individuals and the computer. Shortly, the two of them found themselves in an artificial world. ALU had transferred them to a mountain village as programmed. When the show host woke up in ALU, he was in a state of shock. Robert expected a different reaction. They were transferred in front of a house. That house happened to be the presenter's childhood home. Astonished, he asked, "Is this real?", to which Robert replied, "It depends on how you perceive reality. For me, it is."

The man approached the house, went inside, and told Robert that what they had created was unbelievable. He began to touch the walls of the house, amazed and inhaled deeply. The host felt no difference. The two of them spent some time in the ALU and then they were transferred back to reality.

Almost speechless, he managed to overcome his emotions and shock.

"Ladies and gentlemen, what I have experienced in this moment is incredible and can change the fate of the world," he announced, and the audience cheered and clapped for the team.

At the end of the show, the presenter asked Robert about the plan. Robert responded that the plan would be for anyone to be able to purchase the ALU system starting next week, on Tuesday, June 21, 2101. Him and his team went back to their respective homes.

On his way home, Robert stopped by Alexandra's sister's place to pick up Emma.

The next day, after he dropped Emma off at school, Robert went to his laboratory where he met Darius. Robert opened his laptop, and then a flood of emails started coming in from certain individuals - some from other television networks, and others from curious people interested in the ALU project. He responded to each person, providing explanations and information about the ALU device.

In the following days, Robert was contacted by numerous individuals and companies interested in sponsoring him, but Robert didn't accept anyone outside of his project partners.

The day of the ALU device's release approached quickly, and Robert already had many emails with inquiries from the public about how to purchase a spot in the artificial world. So, before he sold the device to each buyer, Robert called upon Darius, Leo, and Alexandra for a final preparation before they launched the ALU product.

The day of June 21, 2101, arrived, at 12:00, and Robert and his friends gave the green light for sales. Within a few minutes, a flood of purchase requests for the ALU device started to pour in. Buyers would receive the ALU device, designed as a cube, but the cube contained memory and special programs for artificial life. It could be connected to any computer through a single cable.

Robert was very excited because the money they would accumulate could be reinvested in ALU technology.

The ALU device was very easy to install. Buyers just needed to follow the correct instructions provided. So, each client could connect to the ALU device independently, and no assistance would be required. While each buyer would need a power source, the device itself did not require the internet to access the virtual world. It was a unique program where, when a client wanted to access the ALU central, there would be no problem because the ALU cube, i.e., the device, would be directly connected through the IRSS device installed inside the ALU cube. The device functioned as both an internet and Wi-Fi network at the same time.

Before they launched their project for sale, they had made a contract with a company from Japan that specialized in building the ALU device. Robert had become good friends with the Japanese that helped him a year ago. They had told him that if he ever needed any assistance, he should contact them, and Robert did so because he trusted them. The company responsible for building the ALU cube was called Tokyo Innovation Technology. When Robert sold the product, the order would go directly to the company in Japan for production, and they would also handle the delivery. Tokyo Innovation Technology would receive a twenty percent share for each ALU product.

Robert, together with his team and the directors from Japan, created a price list for each ALU product divided into levels:
* Level 1 could be purchased for £3000.
* Level 2 could be purchased for £10,000.
* Level 3 could be purchased for £100,000.

However, it was important to note that each purchased level would have limitations, and if an ALU device owner wanted more, they would have to pay for any customization.

At the end of the day, Robert realized that they had already sold 4560 devices, distributed as follows: 1560 at level 1, 1700 at level 2, and 1300 at level 3. The total calculated amount was £151,680,000 in a single day. When he saw the total sum, Robert couldn't move from his seat, he seemed frozen.

Recovering from the state of shock, Robert stood up from his chair and started to shout with joy. Darius, Leo, and Alexandra embraced him, and all four of them celebrated their success.

Before they headed home, Robert decided to connect to the ALU device to meet with his wife. He shared the news that he had now put his technology up for sale and had already sold a lot of ALU systems. Emily congratulated Robert. He spent some more time with his wife and daughter in the virtual world and then returned to the real world.

Chapter 10

An extraordinary period followed, with sales which increased significantly every day.

Soon, Emma's birthday approached. Robert called an event planning company and organized his daughter's birthday. He invited many people including his aunt, Otilia, and Emily's parents, David and Margaret. At the end of the day, Robert gave a speech in which he said, "God has brought a special person into my life, strong, courageous, and believe me, without this being, I couldn't be the man I am today. And through this moment, I want to convey, through the power of God, that I love her and thank her from the bottom of my heart for giving us our little angel. Now, Emma, you turn 8 years old, and I want you to know that Dad will always be by your side, and I want you to know that I love you immensely."

The next day, after Emma's birthday, Robert was invited to an engineering and innovation gala in London. There, Robert presented his project in front of a crowd, which included a representative of an organ trafficking specialized mafia group. Robert was unaware that someone from that mafia group was present at the gala as well.

After he presented his project, he went outside to smoke a cigarette, and was approached by that individual. He seemed interested in artificial life and its benefits. Unaware of the person standing in front of him, Robert responded that he wanted to offer everyone the opportunity to have a different life, hoping to prevent the wealthy from using the poor population as a source of organs. Then, the anonymous man said, "Aha, so you actually want to stop the mafia groups." Robert affirmed, and after they finished their conversation, the anonymous person asked if they could exchange phone numbers. The individual claimed to be interested in the ALU device as well. Robert didn't hesitate and gave them his phone number.

After the gala, Robert returned home and, on his way to his house, he stopped by his laboratory, where he found Darius. When he entered, Darius smiled and said, "Come quickly to the computer." Then, Darius showed Robert the earnings and told him that the ALU device grew a lot. It had already exceeded 1 billion pounds within a month.

✠

During the following months, sales skyrocketed, and Robert became one of the wealthiest people on the planet.

Their project had changed the future of many individuals worldwide. Robert received numerous emails from certain individuals who wrote to him about how he had transformed their lives. For instance, he received an email from a specific doctor who shared that with the help of the ALU device, he had managed to enhance his wisdom and achieve greater success in his profession.

Robert was thrilled by what he had accomplished so far. His life had dramatically changed. He was no longer an unknown person, but now recognized by many across the globe.

One fine day, before Christmas, Robert connected to the artificial world to visit his virtual family. There, he met his wife and Emma. After an afternoon with the family, Emma had gone to sleep, and Robert remained with Emily.

The two were in the kitchen, and Robert took Emily's right hand in his and kissed it. They hugged and Emily whispered in his ear, "What if we go upstairs to the bedroom and spend some time together?" Robert responded affirmatively, and the two kissed and went to their bedroom. Robert held Emily in his arms and gently laid her on their bed. It had been over a year since they had an intimate connection between their bodies. After some time, once Robert and Emily had satisfied their desires, they went downstairs to the living room. Emily prepared two cups of hot chocolate. After he had spent more time with Emily, Robert returned to reality.

Christmas day arrived and Robert had invited all his close friends and family to the Christmas table.

Later in the evening, Robert received an anonymous phone call. On the other side of the phone call, a male voice, distorted like that of a robot, spoke.

"Hello, who is this?" asked Robert, once he had gone outside to not disturb the others.

"I am someone you will soon get to know," the anonymous caller responded.

"Who the hell are you?" Robert huffed and puffed, tired of the threats he received.

"Well, I am a person who belongs to a powerful family," the caller responded, almost grinning.

"And what does this powerful family have to do with me?" Robert asked, puzzled.

"You are ruining things for us. How come our business is no longer running as smoothly as it used to because of you?" the individual asked, rhetorically.

"How does my activity affect your business?" questioned Robert.

"You know well, Robert. Remember when your wife and daughter were in a coma, and you instantly refused our offer," the person answered, revealing his identity.

Robert recalled the incident when he had to hide because of them.

"What do you want from me?" he asked, anger building up inside of him. He thought he had gotten rid of these individuals.

"We want you to give up on this filthy idea of giving people the opportunity to live in an artificial world," the mafia person threatened.

"Never! And know that I am not afraid of you, and I will not give up on my idea of creating a better world," Robert replied, confidently, and hung up the phone.

Darius saw him pale and worried. He asked Robert if everything was alright, and he told Darius about the phone conversation he just had. His friend called out the callers' bluff, not believing they were gonna hurt Robert, and told him that he should not worry. Nevertheless, deep down in his heart, Robert felt a growing sense of worry, aware of the gravity of the threats and the danger he and his family could be in.

On the day after Christmas, Robert's aunt informed him that she would be staying with him for a while to help with the girl. Her gesture brought him some comfort, knowing that he had her support and protection in this difficult situation.

After the conversation with his aunt, Robert headed determinedly to his laboratory. Once in his office, he sat down, his tired body sinking into the chair, and turned on the computer. As he waited for it to load, he ran his hand through his hair and sighed deeply. His thoughts were clouded with worries and the responsibility of protecting not only his project, but also his family from the threat of the powerful mafia group. He decided he could not remain passive and had to act against the situation. Robert gathered his courage and started devising a meticulous plan. He assessed his resources, identified the mafia's weaknesses, and sought ingenious solutions to counter them. He was aware that every step had to be carefully calculated and every move would influence his and his loved ones' future. Thus, he began to outline his defense strategy, considering every detail and every possible consequence. Determination lit up his eyes and fear was gradually replaced by resolve and the desire to do whatever was necessary to protect his family and project from the threat. Robert knew that the path ahead was difficult and dangerous, but he was determined to fight with all his strength to defend what mattered most to him.

He called Darius to discuss the security and future of their company.

Robert took out a notebook in which he had devised a plan. The idea was to move the company to a different location.

"Do you have a place in mind?", asked Darius, curious about what Robert had come up with this time.

"I have found an island for sale in the Atlantic Ocean, with an area of 1,300 square kilometers. I want to build a powerful corporation. Also, it being located in the middle of the ocean would make it very difficult for us to be attacked or sabotaged by anyone," Robert revealed.

Darius asked Robert how much it cost, and Robert replied that he had spoken with the agency responsible for selling the island, and it was listed for the price of 150 million dollars. His friend was amazed and said that it was a large sum, but considering the size of the island, it wasn't bad. Robert added that in the near future, they would be able to build a protected city for people threatened by the mafia.

Later, Robert also told the others about the company's relocation. Leo and Alexandra supported the idea, and the ALU corporation gradually became very powerful and stable in the months since Robert put the ALU device up for sale. Robert hired several people in various specialized fields to help him maintain his company.

About two weeks after Robert spoke with the agency responsible for selling the island, he scheduled a meeting with them to discuss the purchase plan, and they set the date for 18/02/2102, which happened to fall on a Friday. Robert was eager to go, excited about making the company a safe space and keeping the project hidden from threats.

He prepared in advance with ideas. Robert put in considerable effort to prepare his plan for the relocation and modernization of the corporation, considering important aspects such as ensuring a stable power source for the ALU central facility. He analyzed various options to efficiently power the company, including the use of renewable sources and advanced technologies. Additionally, Robert developed plans for creating an electricity generation system within the ALU corporation, ensuring that operations would continue under optimal conditions even in the event of external power disruptions. He also focused on securing a reliable source of drinkable water for employees and evaluated solutions for proper infrastructure, including the construction of a drinking water supply system and waste management infrastructure.

Through his well-crafted plans, Robert aimed to create a safe, protected, and efficient working environment for employees and to build a strong and sustainable corporation in the near future. During this period of intense preparation, he benefited from the assistance of specialized individuals he had hired to implement these plans for the ALU corporation.

On February 18, 2102, Robert, Darius, Alexandra, and Leo, along with the agents responsible for selling the island, set off for the island in a helicopter rented from the agency. Once there, Robert was fascinated by the beauty of the island and its landscape. They spent a few hours exploring the island, and then returned to the laboratory in Cambridge, where the excitement was felt by everyone. It was there that Robert made the firm decision to acquire the island, and the next day, he met with the agents and signed the purchase agreement. Thus, Robert became the owner of an island and, moreover, achieved a remarkable status in the business world.

Chapter 11

In the following months, Robert hired a construction company to build the ALU corporation complex on the island. The project included the construction of the ALU central building, which would house laboratories, offices, and the central computer. He also made plans for the installation of wind turbines, a solar panel park, and a generator to provide a sustainable energy source. Robert's ideas also included the construction of housing for employees, a harbor for ships, a helipad, and a small airport.

However, Robert's vision went beyond this project, with the ultimate goal of transforming the island into a habitat for millions of people. He dreamed of the island becoming a future place to live for millions of individuals and had grand plans for developing the infrastructure, including the construction of schools, hospitals, shopping centers, and other facilities necessary for a prosperous community.

One day, Robert reconnected to the ALU device. He met with Emily and told her about his plans and the island he had purchased. While he shared all this, he was interrupted by Emily, who seemed to be a little bit on the edge.

"I have news to tell you," she said, tears forming in her eyes.

"What news, darling?" he asked.

She confessed to him that she was pregnant. Upon hearing this, Robert felt confused because he couldn't understand how it was possible.

"It's a miracle, Robert, it's a miracle," she beamed, crying.

She then explained to Robert that she had felt a bit unwell and didn't know why because in the virtual world, you were not supposed to get sick. So she decided to take a test, even though, to her knowledge, this was impossible. When the three minutes of waiting was done, she looked at the test and couldn't believe her eyes. That was how she had found out.

Robert took Emily and little Emma and went to the hospital. When they arrived, a nurse took them and led them to a room to perform a scan on Emily. While the nurse conducted the scan, Robert saw the baby and was filled with joy, but at the same time, he was very confused because he didn't expect such a thing to happen in the virtual world.

Robert asked the nurse how many months it had been. The nurse told Robert that Emily had been pregnant for 7 months and she was expected to give birth in September. Robert and Emily thanked the nurse and then headed home.

At home, Emily asked Robert if he was alright and he answered that he was better than alright, he felt wonderful. Emily continued to reassure him that everything would be alright.

At the end of the day, Robert returned to reality, where Darius was waiting for him. Seeing him lost in thought, Darius asked Robert what was wrong, and Robert told him the news. Darius was surprised and confused. He could not understand how this was even possible. Opening the ALU computer monitor, he started to read all the data created by the A.I. ALU. He discovered that on December 24th, 2101, A.I. ALU had a change in its codes. In fact, the ALU computer independently recreated additions of codes and data to facilitate births. Robert and Darius realized that the ALU device could recreate artificial life and that anyone who had an intimate relationship in the artificial world could have children.

They needed to keep the incident a secret.

Robert's life was changing day by day. The peak of his happiness was that Emily would give birth to their second child during his birthday month. On September 23rd, 2102, Robert would turn the beautiful age of 37.

✠

One day, Robert was contacted by the construction company director. He delivered the news that the constructions would be completed on August 26th, 2102. Robert was overjoyed and immediately picked up the phone to call Alexandra, Darius, and Leo to share the news.

A few days later, they started preparations to move all the technology to the 'new frontier' island, as they had named it.

That day arrived and they loaded all the technology and belongings they had into a truck and headed to Cambridge Airport, where Robert had rented a plane to transport the technology to the new frontier island.

The airport on the island was completed, and all the other projects were finished. Only some final touches remained, but that was not a problem.

Upon arrival, Robert and his team began to unload all the equipment they had brought in the following hours.

The ALU device became active on the new frontier island. Robert was amazed at how his project took shape.

Soon enough, September arrived. Robert would connect to the ALU device daily, until one day, on the 7th of September, Emily told him that she had started to have contractions. Robert and Emily prepared to go to the hospital, leaving Emma with Emily's mother – at this point, Robert and Emily's entire family had been recreated in ALU – and they, excitedly, headed towards the hospital. They reached the destination and went to the reception, where Emily was assigned to a room where she would give birth.

Strangely, the doctors did not participate in any births, but the ALU computer algorithm recreated this special event. The doctors had no suspicion that this birth was not real. The codes and programs created by the ALU computer provided artificial individuals with knowledge as in reality.

Finally, Emily had given birth to a healthy and beautiful baby girl, like a rose. Robert took Emily and the baby in his arms and said, "I can't believe it." Emily kissed Robert and said, "It's real. Robert, you have to think differently, you have to accept this miracle." He responded, saying, "Yes, of course I accept it." He was overjoyed because he had given life to the first baby with artificial intelligence. Robert asked Emily, "What should we name her? How about Luna?" Emily smiled and said, "Welcome home, Luna."

Chapter 12

After spending some time with his family, Robert returned to reality and entered a period of months, during which his life changed every day. He became the richest person in the world and ALU technology was constantly being upgraded with new programs. The ALU device changed the lives of millions of people.

Robert and his colleagues launched the construction of a city on the new frontier island, which would accommodate millions of individuals. However, the people who would reside on the island would be chosen by the team of professionals created by Robert.

Their mission was to bring in individuals in need who had been affected by society, such as those traumatized by criminal groups, political corruption, and other threats.

The construction of the city, named ALU City, was expected to take approximately 8 years. It would include skyscrapers, schools, hospitals, parks, and specially designed areas for children. Robert was also informed by the construction company that the project would be completed in 2110.

Now, all Robert had to do was enjoy the moments he had in reality with his daughter, friends, and colleagues, and in the artificial world with his wife and their two daughters, Emma and Luna.

✠

Years passed, and it was now the year 2109. Emma, in the real world, was 15 years old and had become an independent teenager. Robert had raised her to always have a winning mentality and always find solutions to problems. She had now majored in scientific technology because she grew up in an environment surrounded by engineers and scientists.

Robert's birthday was approaching. Emma had prepared a surprise for him. Together with the scientists on the island, they had been working on two secret projects for her father. 1. Harnessing energy directly from the sun and 2. a project related to synthetic life, which meant creating a synthetic body that resembled a human body.

Emma decided to take on finishing these projects because her father had told her that it was his next plan, two years ago, when she was 13 years old.

On Robert's birthday, Emma set up the two projects in a warehouse on the island to surprise him. Along with Darius, Alexandra, and Leo, she organized a surprise party and made him a cake. Robert was turning 44 years old. Darius went to fetch her father, pretending that he wanted to show him something important, leading him into the warehouse where Emma, along with Robert's entire team, had been waiting to surprise him. As they entered, everyone invited by Emma started shouting, "Happy birthday!" Surprised, he thanked them all and afterwards approached Emma.

"Dad, I have a surprise for you," said Emma enthusiastically. Darius blindfolded Robert with a scarf so that he wouldn't see the surprise beforehand. Emma took his hand and led him to another room in the warehouse where the two projects were set up. Upon entering that room, Emma asked her dad, "Are you ready?" He responded with a smile, "Yes." Emma took off the blindfold, and in that moment, Robert saw the two projects created by Emma. He remained astonished and exclaimed, "This is unbelievable, how did you do this?" Emma explained to Robert, "Dad, I knew how much you wanted these projects to be done, so over the past year, I've been planning to work on them for you because I know how important they are for you." Robert embraced Emma and told her that he loved her very much and was so proud of her.

Some time ago, Robert had talked about how the new frontier island would need a powerful energy source to sustain the island with uninterrupted energy. The energy would be collected from the sun with the help of a specially built satellite designed to approach the sun. When the satellite would reach the correct distance from the sun, it would have to use some instruments to absorb solar radiation, and then it would be transmitted to another satellite orbiting around the planet Earth. The solar-orbiting satellite would collect the energy and then transmit it through controlled solar radiation. The planetary satellite then could receive and transmit it to the storage point created on the new frontier island. There, specially created mechanisms and laboratories would convert this radiation into electricity, enabling the ALU company to power the entire island or the entire planet without any problems. The project was called 'ALU Solar Energy'.

"And it is ready," Darius mentioned, "it will be operational in a few months, on the date 05/03/2110. It will be transported and sent into space with the help of a private space company," he continued.

The second project was something special for Robert, since he had devised a plan to carry out this project but refrained from doing so for the time being.

A year ago, Emma entered Robert's office to take a pen and then noticed the desk drawer was open. Emma pulled the drawer and found some papers with sketches and information about the synthetic body. She took photos of all the sheets and closed the drawer. The detailed explanation of the body was that anyone who didn't want to acquire the ALU device and live in the artificial world would be able to live in the real world in a synthetic body that would look just like a real person. Thus, the synthetic artificial body could be recreated with the desired features of the person who purchased it, in order to represent them. The connection between a person and the synthetic body would only be made when that person would be ill or reached a certain age and had to make that decision. However, it should be noted that individuals who obtained a synthetic body had to give up their real body. The functioning of the synthetic body was achieved through the Artificial Brain device, which contained data copied by nanorobots from the brain of the person who had decided to give up their real body. The energy distribution had to be mentioned in order to keep the source powered, which was done with the help of a specially created device. The device was called 'solar cells', which meant skin, which would cover the synthetic body and would contain specially created cells to directly absorb energy from the sun. Energy had to also be accumulated through nutrition, just like in the case of a real human body when consuming food and water. In the event that the synthetic body ran out of energy, the person who owns it could recharge the body with a specially created device resembling an injection, which contained reserve energy.

When the party with his daughter and team came to an end, Robert asked Emma how she managed to accomplish these projects. She explained to him that she succeeded with the help of the ALU device, because she constantly connected to the artificial world and studied these projects until she succeeded. Robert congratulated Emma and said, 'Well done, my daughter!'

Afterwards, Robert went to the central laboratory where the central ALU was installed. There, he connected to an ALU device and transferred himself to the artificial world, because he wanted to spend some time with his wife and their two daughters, Emma and Luna.

Upon arriving home in the artificial world, Robert was welcomed by his family, and his three special loved ones wished him a happy birthday. Robert embraced Emma, and at that moment, he felt a little strange because he had been keeping this secret for many years, the fact that Emma was alive.

However, the problem was that, one day, Robert would have to tell Emily that their daughter had recovered from the coma, and he had kept the secret for so many years. Robert would not tell Emily soon because it was not the right time.

He took Luna in his arms, and she wished him a happy birthday, laughing and giggling.

Robert, Emily, Emma, and Luna went to a restaurant in the city.

On the way, Robert looked around and noticed how much the artificial world was becoming real because the ALU codes were constantly being adapted.

After having dinner together, they returned home. Robert stayed alone for a while, and after his daughters fell asleep, he transferred himself back to reality.

In the following period of time, Robert lived a normalcy between reality and virtuality. Emma grew day by day, and the ALU corporation had become very powerful. Robert had thousands of people working for him, because the ALU corporation was not only concerned with the artificial world or the artificial universe. At the same time, Robert's company created many other projects that helped humanity.

Money was not a problem. He had enough funds to create any project he desired.

In a few months, the ALU city was set to be completed. It was remarkable for Robert, considering he managed to fulfill his ambitious plan in less than 10 years. Everything was progressing at a perfect pace.

At the same time, Robert also funded another project, ALU Space, which was soon to begin construction. ALU Space would be responsible for sending satellites into space and astronaut teams.

However, Robert's plans did not stop there. He planned to create a space station where he could install the central ALU to keep it safe. For now, though, this plan had to wait until the other projects were completed.

Chapter 13

Finally, after a few months, the day of the inauguration of the ALU city arrived. Robert invited a multitude of important individuals, such as heads of state, prime ministers, and other influential people from around the world. He set up a stage in front of the ALU institution, where thousands of people gathered.

Robert addressed the crowd with a speech, but before he began, a large screen was installed on the stage, and he projected an emotional video on it. It started depicting the current state of the planet. During this time, planet Earth faced drastic climate changes, poverty was at an alarming level, and corruption and crime were prevalent. After the video ended, Robert began his speech by saying, "Ladies and gentlemen, together with the ALU corporation, we have created this city to make a change in this world, to help millions of people find refuge or enhance their wisdom through the ALU device. I refuse to accept that individuals with low income or health issues should be adversely affected by other societies, such as the wealthy or mafia groups." Robert further mentioned how it was possible for people with health problems or poverty to be exploited as a source of human organ exchange by the mafia for the benefit of the wealthy society.

At the end, he was applauded by the entire crowd who attended the event.

Robert stepped down from the stage and approached his friends, Darius, Alexandra, and Leo, saying, "I thank you from the bottom of my heart for everything you have done for me and for your support and sacrifices. Know that without you, I wouldn't have been able to fulfill this dream of mine."

The four of them embraced and jumped with joy.

The ALU corporation had taken shape and wielded great influence globally. Robert was in a good position now, considering that when he embarked on this journey, he had no idea he would be able to succeed, but hope and his resilient character, along with the support of those close to him, helped him navigate this path successfully.

Until the year 2111, Robert managed to gather over 6 million residents on New Frontier Island.

He successfully completed all the plans for building the island as he had envisioned and started the project related to the space station that would house the central ALU computer. The space station would be a closely guarded secret, as Robert did not not want to disclose its location or how its construction would look.

Over the coming years, Robert would send rockets with astronauts and specially built robots for this type of mission.

Firstly, Robert would construct a fake space station near Earth, with the idea of misleading anyone, so that he could secretly hide the construction of the real space station, which would be built in Jupiter's orbit. The engineers and scientists at ALU Space had created rockets with extraordinary speed, which reached nearly 70% of the speed of light, capable of reaching Jupiter in approximately 50 minutes. The engine was currently in testing and experts confirmed it would be ready soon. Robert aimed for both the fake and real space stations to begin construction in the year 2113. The space station would be called 'Roots of Earth' and would have the shape of a small planet, with a size of 20 thousand square kilometers. Inside, it would also contain a small city where astronauts and the personnel taking care of the station could live. After the completion of the construction of this space station, the central ALU inside it could be connected to all the other ALU devices on Earth or vice versa. It would be possible with the help of the luminous Radio Shock Source (IRSS) communication system.

✠

One day, Robert went into his office and locked himself in. He took out an album of photographs, identical to the one he had given to Emma when she was hospitalized. As he looked through the album, Robert smiled and cherished those moments.

He realized it was time to reveal his secrets to Emma about her mother. However, Robert faced a dilemma. The virtual Emma, who was also celebrating her 18th birthday. Complication arose from the fact that, if the real Emma connected to the ALU device where her replica lived, the artificial Emma would disappear. Robert was worried because his artificial daughter had already developed her own memories and wisdom. Nevertheless, Robert considered all the consequences and decided to tell Emma the truth.

So, he called Emma and asked if they could meet on the island's promenade. She agreed, and an hour later, they met. Robert had bought two coffees and they sat down on a bench.

"I called you here because I would like to tell you something very important. Actually, a secret, about your mother," Robert started.

"What secret, dad?" Emma asked, intrigued about the fact that her dad wanted to share something about her mother who had passed away when she was a small child.

"My dear daughter, in a few days, you will turn 18, and I have decided that it is time to reveal a secret that I have kept from you since you were 7 years old," he continued," but fist, please believe me that I did not intend to hide this secret forever. I waited for the right moment, and that moment is now. Do you remember when we scattered your mother's ashes?" Robert began to feel a knot forming in his chest.

"Yes, I remember," replied Emma.

"Well, I want you to know that when your mother was in a coma and we couldn't find a way to bring her back to life, I decided to copy her memory cells using the AB device. Since then, your mother has been living in the virtual world, and she doesn't know that you have come out of the deep coma. I didn't want to tell her that you had awakened, so as not to emotionally affect her in the artificial world. I also want to tell you that there is a replica of you in the virtual world, who is now the same age as you, and that replica has built new memories in the virtual world, but that's not all."

Robert also explained to Emma that she had another sister named Luna, who was the first child born in the artificial world.

When Emma heard all of this, she started crying and asked Robert why he had lied to her. He tried to embrace her, but Emma pushed him.

"Leave me alone!" she shouted.

"Forgive me, I didn't mean for this to happen!" Robert attempted to calm her down, begging.

68

Emma got up from the bench and ran back to the house.

"Please forgive me, please stay!" Robert called after her, pleading, but she didn't stop.

Later that evening, Robert went to Emma's bedroom door. He knocked and asked, "Emma, can I come in?" She replied, "Yes," and he entered. Emma had smudged makeup from crying. Robert sat on the bed beside her and said, "I know you're angry with me, but my only chance of earning your forgiveness is to prove that I didn't keep your mother away from you intentionally."

At one point, Emma began to cry and jumped into her father's arms.

"I'm sorry for my reaction, but I want to ask you if I can see Mommy and my sister Luna, even though they're not real," she asked, hope filling her eyes.

"Of course, my angel, but before we take that step, we need to calm down and discuss it because there's a small problem. When you connect to the ALU device, your replica will be restricted, " explained Robert patiently.

"What do you mean?" Emma asked, confusion starting to form on her face.

She had connected many times to the artificial world. No one had told her that it could have such grave consequences.

"Yes, that's true," Robert responded, "but you haven't connected to the ALU computer where your mother's world is created. And you should also know that the world your mother lives in is not connected to the central ALU. However," Robert informed Emma, "the decision to see your mother is up to you".

The next day, Emma went to see her father in his office.

"Are you alright, my dear?" Robert asked her, bringing his head a little bit out of the computer.

"Yes, dad, I'm fine," she exclaimed, taking a seat on the other side of his desk, waiting patiently for Robert to finish what he was working on.

"How can I help you?" he asked, curious about her visit.

"I've made a decision and I have an idea. I obviously don't want to destroy my replica in the artificial world, but there is an alternative that would allow me to connect to the ALU device without causing any issues to my replica."

"How?" Robert looked at Emma, his focus completely on her. He hadn't yet discovered a way that would fix this issue.

"I would have to use the AB device to recopy my entire memory. After that, I will only need to modify certain codes, which will allow two people to have the same DNA in the artificial world," she explained thoroughly, not leaving any details out of her plan.

Robert approved of the idea and asked her when she would like to take this step. Emma would have started on it at that moment. She was so eager to see her mother, but they made plans to get it done the next day.

Emma left Robert alone in his office. He went to connect to the ALU computer. Darius was there too, waiting for Robert. He told Darius that he had come forth to Emma about her mother, Luna, and her replica, and now she wanted to see them. However, before Emma met them, Robert wanted to tell Emily the secret he had kept from her regarding Emma. Darius put the ALU device on Robert's head and then entered the connection codes between Robert and the computer, transferring him to the artificial world.

As he approached the house, Robert thought about how he would tell Emily and the girls.

He opened the door and Emma and Luna were sitting on the living room couch, watching television. Emma saw him and called, "Hi, dad! Did you finish work early today?"

"Hello, my dear! Yes, I finished early," he replied, smiling at them.

Luna got up from the couch and ran towards him, hugged him, and said, "Dad, you know that soon Emma will turn 18. And I will be 9 in two months!" He smiled and said affectionately, obviously he was joking, "Oh, I forgot, but thank you for reminding me. I don't know what I would do without you, Luna."

"Oh, dad, you can be so forgetful sometimes," she laughed, returning to the couch and taking a seat next to her older sister.

Robert heard his wife laughing from the kitchen and walked in her direction.

"Good day, my love, how are you?" He asked, kissing her cheeks.

"I'm fine, thank you, but why are you here so early? You usually come in the evenings," she asked, puzzled.

"My love, I would like to discuss something very important," he urged, leading Emily towards their terrace, at the back of the house.

Robert acknowledged that what he was about to say would shock her.

Thoughtfully, Emily responded, "What news do you have that would shock me, my love?"

"Do you remember the day when I made the decision to copy your memory and Emma's with the help of the AB device," he asked, nervously.

"Yes, of course I remember. How could I forget such an important day?" Emily answered, a smile forming on her face.

"I'm glad you embedded that day in your memories," said Robert, "but I want to confess something that happened on that day. After you were permanently recreated in the artificial world, I came back to do the same procedure with Emma, but something occurred that I kept secret from you all these years."

"What secret?" queried Emily, her facial expression starting to change.

"When I returned to reality after successfully recreating you here in the artificial world, our daughter, Emma, woke up from a coma. She is alive," blurted Robert, not knowing what to expect from Emily.

When she heard the news, she froze and couldn't utter a word.

Chapter 14

After Emily recovered from the shock of the news she received, she screamed at Robert, "Why didn't you tell me the truth, you liar?", tears running down her face.

"Yes, I know I lied, but understand, it wasn't easy for me to keep this secret hidden. Please, I beg you, forgive me!" he pleaded, sitting on his knees in front of his wife.

"So, Emma didn't know anything until yesterday? What do you mean?" Emily asked, feeling the betrayal even deeper.

"It's hard to explain why I didn't tell her from the beginning. As you know, she was very young, and you also know that we made the same decision with Emma's replica," Robert replied. He was trying to find a middle ground, a way his wife would understand his choices.

"What am I going to tell my daughter here, in the artificial world? What will happen to her?" she asked him.

Robert explained to her that he and the real Emma have a plan that will be put into action tomorrow, after discussing it for some time. Emily, beginning to somewhat understand Robert's intentions, said, "And now we have to explain all of this to this Emma as well." They both were concerned, not knowing how she would react.

Emily went and called her daughter outside. Emma sat next to her father, not anticipating the news she was about to receive. News that would change her life forever, most probably.

"Is everything alright?" she asked them. Emma could read their emotions well; she knew something wasn't right.

"Yes, my dear daughter, everything is just fine. However, I do have a secret that I have kept hidden from you for so long," Robert admitted.

And so, he began to explain everything that had happened, from the day of the accident in 2100 until the present. After Emma found out that she was a replica of a person from the real world, she said thoughtfully,

"So, everything in this world is fake, including me. Did you know about this?" she asked Emily.

"Yes, I knew, but your father and I made this decision together at that time because you were too young," Emily confessed.

"And what will happen to me?" she asked, "Will I be deleted from this world?"

"No, dear," Robert said, "You should know that the real Emma can't wait to see you, and she has done everything possible for the codes and the ALU device in the artificial world to accept two people with the same DNA".

Emily, looking at her daughter affectionately, told her, "My dear, I know these revelations are overwhelming and make you feel unsure about your own existence, but you must understand that you are more than just a mere replica of another girl. You have a distinct personality, your own experiences, and you are loved here in the artificial world."

Emma wiped away a tear and asked in a trembling voice, "But if I'm just a copy, what's the meaning of it all? Why should I continue to live in this artificial world?"

Robert, looking at his wife and daughter, warmly responded, "My dear, the meaning of your life is not determined by your origin or the world you live in. The meaning of life is created by the experiences you have, the connections you form, and how you choose to truly live."

Emily intervened, "Emma, each of us has a purpose and unique value in this world. It doesn't matter where we come from or how we were created. You are a special person with potential and a life to live in this world. Embrace your identity and seek what makes you happy and fulfilled."

Emma reflected on her parents' words and realized that despite the unusual circumstances, she had the power to build her own story and find her purpose in life, even if she was not in the real world. With renewed determination, she looked at her parents and said, "I want to discover who I truly am and live in harmony with the world I'm in. I embrace this journey and I want to do everything possible to connect and get to know the real Emma in the real world."

Robert and Emma looked at her with pride, knowing that Emma would find her own path and accomplish extraordinary things, regardless of the world she was in. Together, they vowed to always be by her side in the journey of self-discovery and to support each other in every step of the way.

In the end, Robert called her sister, Luna. Emma had asked her parents to also tell Luna what she herself had just learned. The surprise was that Luna, considering she was still young at 9 years old, had an advanced mindset in understanding, knowledge, and wisdom. When Luna went outside and the three of them, her sister Emma, her mother, and her father, told her everything from the beginning and explained how she came into the world, Luna responded that she knew how the artificial world worked and what her purpose was. She also told them that she did not believe this was a disadvantage, because she was an AI child. She added that, in the future, there would be many ways to connect with the real world.

Robert was amazed by the wisdom of his daughter, Luna, and responded by telling her that her sister, Emma, and he were working on a similar project called 'synthetic body'. Luna seemed to be pretty excited for the outcome of the project. Referring to her sister in the artificial world, she emphasized that it didn't matter that she was a replica, because it would not make a difference.

After discussing and recounting everything that had happened in both parts of the world, Luna suggested that they needed to find a way not to confuse Emma from reality and Emma from the artificial world. With a smile on her face, showcasing how clever she was, Emma calmly and peacefully responded to her thoughts, "What if I call myself Emma AI from now on? And we let the real Emma keep the name Emma because I like the name Emma AI."

Robert and his wife approved Emma's request to be named Emma A.I.

Everyone was content with the idea that they were who they were. After that, they further discussed how to welcome Emma tomorrow when she connected to the ALU device.

The end of the day arrived, and Robert embraced and kissed his two girls on the cheek, and then went to Emily and said, "I love you, my love, and thank you for understanding me."

Afterwards, Robert returned to the real world. He explained everything he had told his family to Darius.

The next morning, Robert met his daughter Emma at the laboratory where he would perform the memory transfer between the real and artificial worlds. After Emma's entire memory was copied, Robert approached her and said, "I know it was hard for you to accept that I lied to you for so long, but know that it was worth it. Now, we will connect you to the ALU device, where your mother and sisters live, and I want you to know that I will be by your side."

Robert also connected to the ALU device and gave the green light to Darius that they were ready to be transferred to the artificial world. He was thrilled that he had finally told the truth and his family would finally be reunited in the artificial world.

Arriving in the artificial world, Emma and Robert approached their house. There, they were greeted by Emily, together with her two daughters.

Upon seeing Robert and Emma entering the house, Emily rushed towards Emma and excitedly exclaimed, "My daughter, I can't believe it! Your father told me a lot of things about you and I want you to know that I am so proud of you, Emma," said Emily, looking into her daughters' eyes.

"Mommy, I missed you so much," cried Emma, taking Emily into a big hug.

"I know, my daughter, I know. But it's never too late. We're together now," Emily cried tears of happiness.

After embracing her real daughter, Emily said, "Let me introduce you to Luna."

They hugged, excited they would get to know each other. Luna, like a mischievous child, said with a smile on her face, "Now I have to explain things to two sisters, not just one."

With a smile, Emily mentioned that she wanted to introduce her to her replica, Emma AI. Emma and Emma AI got closer to each other and started smiling and laughing.

"I'm extremely pleased to meet you," said Emma to Emma A.I. After getting to know each other and talking, Emma, Luna, and Emma AI went out into town.

Robert and Emily remained at home. The two of them sat at the table, beaming with content. They were so happy over how smoothly the meeting had gone. Emily asked Robert what would happen next, and he explained that, from that moment on, they would see each other more often and spend more time together.

At the end of the day, Robert and Emma returned to reality. Emma got up from the bed she was sitting on and smiled at Robert, "Thank you, Dad."

On Emma's and Emma A.I. 's birthday, Robert, Emma, Darius, Leo, and Alexandra all connected to the ALU device and celebrated the girls' coming of age together. Robert was overjoyed to see the family reunited and his best friends all together in a world he created many years ago.

After the party, Robert, along with his family and friends, opened the portal that connected ALU Central and ALU Home. They all crossed the threshold of the portal and instantly entered another limitless artificial world. They spent some time in ALU Central, where Emily and her daughters were amazed by what Robert had been able to create in the virtual world. After spending some time with their family in ALU, Robert, Emma, and their friends returned to reality.

The next day, on his way to his laboratory, Robert didn't go straight to work because he decided to take a tour of New Frontier Island to see how things were going with all the projects he had implemented on the island.

Later, he returned to his office, made himself a cup of coffee, and sat down at his computer. He took a pen and a sheet of paper from the desk drawer and began listing all the projects he had implemented on the island, including the artificial universe in ALU. The programs installed by Robert and his team allowed anyone to live their life in the artificial world and create loved ones in ALU without needing the consciousness of that person. Simply put, the engineers and programmers would input data and codes that would enable the created individuals to have memories from reality and create their own memories. However, the memories from reality would be limited, while in ALU, they could constantly create new memories.

Chapter 15

In the following years, until the year 2118, Robert managed to successfully complete the secret 'Roots of Earth' space station project and installed the entire memory and AI technology of ALU on the station. The station was technologically advanced. It contained a specially created base for the spacecraft created by ALU Space company, where they were able to land. ALU AI was out of any danger and the 'Roots of Earth' had a very large habitat inside it, where engineers, scientists, and various groups of professionals lived. The 'Roots of Earth' space station transmitted signals at a speed of light-years, so there was no issue of connecting each ALU Home with ALU Central, which was located in the space station.

Robert's influence on the planet Earth was enormous, as Earthlings depended on his facilities and his company. The company supplied 90% of the planet's electricity. The ALU Corporation had heavily invested in recent years in environmental protection, replanting over a billion trees, cleaning the oceans of waste and garbage, as well as building new hospitals, schools, and orphanages.

However, Robert had not managed to change the mindset of corrupt individuals, dirty politicians, or mafia groups that harmed the population. In the eyes of these scammers, Robert was not seen in a positive light. They wanted the ALU corporation to cease its activities, but Robert refused to accept this under any circumstances. He was terrorized every day. The threats consisted of constant phone calls, emails, and letters. Some of them were as brutal as threatening to kill him and his family.

However, faced with these events, Robert made a major decision to protect his family and the ALU corporation. Robert understood that the threats against him and his family were serious, and he couldn't stand idly by. Therefore, he hired a professional security team to protect his loved ones and ensure the safety of the ALU corporation.

He collaborated with authorities, providing them with all relevant information about the threats and suspects. He filed complaints with the police and fully cooperated in ongoing investigations. He also sought the support of the company's IT department to strengthen their cybersecurity and prevent potential attacks on the corporation. Furthermore, Robert encouraged his employees to be vigilant and report any suspicious activity. He organized training sessions to teach them how to recognize and respond to potential dangers.

Three years ago, Robert came up with the idea of building a massive concrete wall offshore, two kilometers away from the island's shore. The wall was constructed to protect the island. The surrounding wall had three entrances.

Robert had done everything possible to keep millions of refugees away from scammers.

Robert and his family had lived in both the real world and the artificial world in recent years, having a happy and enthusiastic life. However, Robert's life was constantly exposed to risk because, unintentionally, he made many enemies, including leaders of countries who were completely against Robert's initiative to create a healthy and protected world. Nevertheless, he managed to overcome any obstacle.

The year 2119 had arrived, and the ALU company would celebrate 19 years since the first ALU AI device was created. Robert would organize a festive party, but at the same time, he would also be celebrating Luna's birthday with his family.

Robert was to spend time with his colleagues on 07/09/2119 and then connect to the ALU device to meet and celebrate Luna's birthday with his family in the artificial world. She was going to turn 17 years old.

Emma, Emma AI, Emily, and Luna had planned a surprise for Robert. The four of them had been secretly working on a project that no one expected.

On the 19th anniversary of the first ALU AI device, Robert invited a lot of important people to the party he organized. The party was being held in the celebration hall of the New Frontier Island palace. There, Robert met his friends, Darius, Alexandra, and Leo. When they saw each other and spoke, they were very happy. At one point, Alexandra said, "Can you believe that 19 years ago we were hiding and didn't know what we were doing? But now look at us, celebrating an important day in all of our lives."

After they spoke, Darius asked, "Where is Emma?" Robert replied, "She should be here before 8:00 PM, I told her we will be giving a speech." He picked up his phone and called her, but she didn't answer. It was 7:57 PM, and in three minutes, Robert and Emma were supposed to deliver the speech. The clock struck 8:00 PM and Robert stepped onto the stage. Deep down, however, he was worried about Emma's whereabouts.

"19 years ago, today, together with Darius, Alexandra, and Leo, we managed to create something extraordinary—the ALU computer, a world in which anyone can live or enjoy freedom. In this world, you can be yourself, create new memories, develop intelligence, and much more. This artificial world has no limits. My wife was the first person created in this world, along with the replica of our daughter, Emma," started Robert. "My daughter was supposed to be up here with me today. I suppose she might be nervous," he said, laughing, "hopefully, we'll see her later." He took a quick pause. "I want to thank everybody who was able to make it here today. It means the world to me and everyone in this company."

Robert continued with his speech and, at the end, thanked everyone again for their support. Lost in thought, as he finished speaking, he turned around and was about to step down from the stage when he heard the commotion behind him. He turned around and was greeted with the sight of his family. Robert stood frozen when he saw them, and when he regained composure, he ran towards them.

"This can't be true!" he exclaimed.

"It was Luna's idea to create synthetic bodies identical to them. We've been working on this surprise for a year now, together with Darius, Alexandra, and Leo. They helped us, along with ALU engineers and specialists," Emma said, explaining everything to Robert.

Robert had tears in his eyes. He embraced his family and said, "I love you so much. Thank you for having the courage to come into the real world and surprise me like this." Luna chimed in and said, "See, Dad? I told you there would be a chance for us to be reunited in both the real and artificial worlds."

After they talked and savored the moment, Robert climbed on a table and shouted, "Dear guests and colleagues, I want to introduce you to my wife, Emily, and our three daughters, Emma, Luna, and Emma AI!" At that moment, the entire audience applauded and rejoiced together with them, for what they had accomplished over the years, considering the immense struggles Robert and his family had faced at the beginning of their journey.

After the party, Robert and his family went home. There, they sat down and talked for hours.

Robert asked Emma how difficult it had been to create the synthetic bodies. He hadn't created any synthetic bodies yet. The only synthetic body was the one Emma had given him as a gift for his birthday a few years ago. Emma explained how she managed to build the bodies of her sisters and her mother. She continued by describing how she inputted the DNA of the three individuals into the database of the device responsible for creating the synthetic body. She inputted the DNA codes copied from the ALU computer database and the AB device. That way, she managed to create the necessary DNA to build bodies identical to the real ones.

"After the construction of the bodies was completed, I duplicated mom's and Emma's A.I. artificial brain. Then, I attached the duplicate of the AB device to the synthetic body and waited for the body to reach the necessary energy to come to life. When the body accumulated enough energy to revive, AB sent information to each organ of the body, so that each organ could start functioning," she explained, happy to see how excited her father was.

"How did you do that with Luna?" Robert asked, curious of what his daughter came up with.

"With Luna, I had to recreate a separate connection system which allowed entry into the synthetic body. In fact, I created a transmitter using the IRSS transmission device, through which Luna directly connects to the artificial brain of the synthetic body," Emma continued, answering all of Roberts' questions.

With the new connectivity system implemented, the Moon was now able to directly connect to the artificial brain of the synthetic body. This allowed her to control and feel the body with ease, as if it were her own. Once the body had accumulated enough energy, an electric wave passed through every fiber and component, bringing it to life. The synthetic body breathed and moved in a way that seemed almost human.

Luna had felt an explosion of emotions and curiosity within her. She was truly free to explore and experience the world from a human perspective. However, there was also a burden of responsibility upon her.

Emma joyfully embraced Luna and said, "Now you are with us, Luna. You are part of our family, and we will do everything we can to support you in this new stage of your life."

Robert was still amazed by what had happened.

"Luna, it's hard for me to understand all of this, but if you are happy and safe, then we are all happy. We will adapt together and do everything we can for you," he said, hugging his daughter.

Since then, Luna continued her journey in her synthetic body, experiencing the world from a completely new perspective. With the support of her family and the desire to discover her own potential, Luna began to build her own identity and explore what it meant to be human in an artificial body.

Chapter 16

Finally, Robert had his entire family by his side and felt stronger than ever.

Days, weeks, and months passed, and now in the year 2119, Robert reached the age of 54. This did not demoralize him at all, as he felt very capable and healthy.

The ALU corporation managed to build safe havens all over the world, for individuals affected by other societies. These safe havens provided people with a secure and protected place to seek refuge and receive the help they needed in the face of difficulties and threats.

Robert and his team worked hard to reach this goal of theirs, ensuring they were equipped with adequate resources, advanced security systems, and access to vital information.

In each safe haven, people found shelter, food, water, and medical care. They were also provided with educational resources to develop their skills and knowledge, allowing them to adapt to a new environment and build a better future.

Robert was proud of his work and the positive impact it had on people's lives. ALU had become a force of stability and hope in a tumultuous world.

Over time, the ALU corporation expanded the safe havens into more remote areas and developed advanced technologies to cope with growing challenges. They collaborated with local communities and humanitarian organizations to create a global network of support and mutual aid.

One day, Robert and his team received surprising news.

Luna, now familiar with life in her synthetic body, had come up with a revolutionary idea to improve the safe havens. She proposed integrating advanced virtual reality simulation technologies into these places, to provide people with the opportunity to experience new worlds and develop their skills in a safe and controlled environment. Robert was impressed by Luna's creativity and vision and immediately approved the implementation of this idea.

They worked together to bring this innovation to the safe havens, offering people the chance to explore their potential and find new ways to reconnect with the outside world.

Thus, the safe havens became places of transformation and personal growth, where people could find safety, community, and resources to build a better future.

Robert, Luna, and the entire ALU team continued to work together, putting their energy and knowledge in the service of humanity, to create a brighter future for all.

✠

One evening, Robert was in his laboratory.

Suddenly, he heard a loud explosion. He quickly got up from his chair and rushed to the window of his office, looking out. In the distance, he could see a massive fire. Robert immediately grabbed his phone and called the security team commander. He asked him what had happened. The commander explained to Robert that there had been an attack at one of the gates of the protective wall, carried out by a kamikaze drone. Robert asked the commander if there were any casualties, and he replied negatively, saying that there were only material damages that could be repaired. He sighed in relief and ordered the evacuation of the entire population on the island to specially equipped bunkers or to transfer themselves virtually into the artificial world of the ALU central, located on the Earth's Roots space station.

As a result, people were directed towards the safety bunkers or entered a virtual reality created in the ALU central. This measure was taken to protect the population and ensure their survival in the face of possible future attacks.

Shortly after, Robert received an anonymous phone call, a male voice on the other end. The caller told Robert to shut down the ALU corporation, or else today's attack would be repeated.

After he hung up, Robert called his friends for an emergency meeting. The meeting was attended by the entire staff responsible for the safety of New Frontier Island. During the meeting, Luna asked if she could address the group, as she had a plan. Robert agreed, and Luna began to outline all her plans. Everyone present was astounded as she mentioned that the ALU corporation could create anti-missile shields and radars to detect any approaching objects near the island. Emma also presented the idea that the island would need mounted weapons on its walls, such as machine guns, to protect the walls in case someone attempted to breach the gate.

Robert was very proud that his daughters took their own initiative and came up with these plans, which he appreciated.

The commander asked when everything would be ready, and they replied that all the military defense equipment would be ready in two weeks, at the most.

In the following weeks, the defense system proposed by Robert's daughters was installed and fully operational.

As Robert was with his family in ALU, together, they came to a decision – to create a secret army of synthetic soldiers.

When he returned to reality, Robert shared the plan with Darius. He asked Robert how they would carry out the recruitment process and Robert came up with the idea of creating a digital platform where anyone who wished, could enroll in this military program, and the soldiers' training would take place in the virtual world.

After deciding all this, the next day, Robert sent an email to all the people living on the island or in the refuge points established by the corporation around the world. The idea was that Robert didn't want to force anyone to participate in this recruitment program, he wanted everyone to have a choice.

The following day, Emma approached her father and said, "Dad, have you seen how many people have enrolled in the recruitment program?"

"No, how many are there?" he asked.

He was curious how many people really cared for the community's safety.

"Over 1 million volunteers," Emma told him.

When Robert heard this, he said, "I didn't want us to reach this point, but it's the only way to protect millions of Earthlings and the ALU corporation."

Emma suggested that Luna should lead the army of synthetic soldiers because she possessed wisdom, courage, and fearlessness. Robert accepted Emma's suggestion and planned to discuss this with Emily and Luna in the evening.

While Robert and Emma were at home, preparing dinner, the synthetic bodies of Emma AI, Luna, and Emily were in standby mode in a separate room, connected to the power source. Suddenly, all three bodies activated. Emily and their two daughters had connected from ALU to their synthetic bodies. It was a common occurrence, as they would often transition from the virtual world to reality due to the seamless connection between ALU and their synthetic bodies.

In the meantime, in the ALU world, a team of cybersecurity professionals was established to protect the integrity and security of the system. These experts were specially trained in detecting and countering cyber threats. The team consisted of specialists with diverse expertise, such as software engineers, security analysts, network experts, and cryptographers. They worked closely with software developers and system architects to ensure that all ALU applications and programs were protected against cyber-attacks. Their main responsibility was to identify and prevent any potential threats to the ALU system. If someone attempted to create a virus that could affect the ALU, the team would need to detect this threat before the virus was introduced into the ALU programs. To accomplish this, they employed advanced techniques for network monitoring and software code analysis.

The team had access to their central location in the ALU, where the AI Brain Anti-Virus was located. It was an advanced artificial intelligence system, specially created and designed by Luna, to detect and combat cyber threats in the artificial world. Through regular updates, the AI Brain Anti-Virus could identify any anomalies or suspicious behavior and thoroughly investigating them. The team's mission was crucial for the safety and stability of the ALU. Through their concerted efforts and expertise in cybersecurity, they ensured that ALU users enjoyed a secure and protected environment while venturing into the artificial world.

Luna played an extraordinary role in developing the surrounding environment in the artificial universe. She had an additional advantage over anyone and anything.

Chapter 17

In recent times, Robert had been frequently threatened every day, and ALU was under cyber-attacks daily. However, Luna's antivirus was performing well and stopped any attack.

After the first kamikaze drone attack, the population on the island started to really panic. Robert, however, did not sit idle, and he, along with his family and friends, were always one step ahead, thus managing to maintain peace on the island during the following years.

In the year 2122, mafia groups, together with countries led by dictators and corrupt officials, began to attack the refuge points around the world.

One of the five refuge bases located in South America was attacked. Around 185 thousand people, including children, women, and men, had taken refuge there. The refuge had soldiers, but unfortunately, they couldn't withstand the wave of attacks from the mafia groups. The mafia took all the remaining residents of this refuge base hostage. At the same time, thousands of people died due to rocket and bomb attacks.

However, before their deaths, some of the residents managed to copy their memories, consciousness, and brain cells using the Artificial Brain device. The AB device was connected to the central computer of ALU, a virtual augmented reality network. The individuals who had copied their consciousness and memories were now safely aboard the space station 'Roots of Earth', orbiting around Jupiter.

The space station was designed as a secure refuge for those who chose to preserve their identity and experiences in the ALU. There, the individuals continued to live in a virtual environment, interacting with other users and exploring digital worlds. Although they no longer had physical bodies, they retained the memories and knowledge accumulated during their real lives.

When Robert learned about the situation at the base in South America, he was very angry and upset. Immediately, he ordered the gathering of synthetic soldiers.

He had managed to build an army of 500,000 synthetic soldiers, each with a replicated brain based on a real one. The soldiers were permanently connected to the ALU system.

Certain soldiers who enlisted in Robert's army had either died due to incurable diseases or advanced age. They had decided to transfer their consciousness into the AB device and then into the ALU. Other soldiers were still alive but could connect to synthetic bodies through two phases.

Phase 1 involved connecting the body to the ALU, while Phase 2 allowed the connection of consciousness to the new synthetic body.

Thus, Robert formed a powerful and diverse army, composed of synthetic soldiers with replicated brains and living soldiers connected to synthetic bodies. The soldiers worked together to confront the threat in South America and to free the hostages taken by the local mafia.

In just 12 hours, Robert had managed to liberate and bring all the captured hostages to safety with the help of his soldiers, led by Luna.

After all the hostages were brought to the island by Luna's army, she went to report to her father. Her report stated that it had been a bloody operation, and that all those who opposed the army had been eliminated. Robert embraced his daughter and thanked her. "Luna, you and your sisters will be true leaders."

After the attack in South America, Robert was informed that other refugee bases had also started to be attacked, however Luna informed him that these bases had successfully defended themselves because they now had well-trained synthetic soldiers and very good military equipment. Robert felt more relieved hearing this news, especially since he learned about it that evening.

On that day, Robert and his family met in the virtual world, where there was peace and harmony, and he could enjoy some quiet. Even though in 2122 Robert was 57 years old, when he was in the ALU, he looked like he was 35 years old, because the programs and codes installed in ALU were permanently set to the age of 35, and he could never age. It was something incredible.

Robert and his family sat at the table and had dinner together. During dinner, Emily said, "I can't believe how bad the world is. Instead of living in harmony and respect, helping each other, we are actually killing each other. The greed for money is huge". Emily asked Robert what would happen next and if he would have to fight these idiots all the time. When she looked at him, something else seemed to have taken over his mind.

"What is on your mind darling?" she asked.

"To be honest, I'm concerned," Robert replied, "statistics show that human organ trafficking is increasing daily, still. Even though we have given the rich the opportunity to connect to ALU, there are still some who do not accept this and prefer to use the poor as organ donors. But another problem is that this year the statistics show that over one billion people live in extreme poverty, without food, water, shelter, and education. These poor people are easily manipulated and used as slaves. My worry is that soon many countries will give up the current energy source we distribute, and other facilities offered by the corporation because they are led by corrupt politicians. But there is also a good side to this world," he said, hopeful," there are other countries that support us in what we do."?

"Which countries are these? That support us?' asked Emma, curiously.

"45% of the countries are from Europe, 36% from Asia, 32% North America, 30% from Africa, 30% from Australia, including New Zealand, partially, and 29% South America."

Emily was slightly surprised by the scale of what Robert said. She was delighted to learn that there were countries supporting their cause and fighting against corruption. However, concern about poverty and human exploitation remained on her mind.
"But what can we do about this situation?" Emily asked, with a determined look, eager to make a change. "How can we help these poor people and put an end to human trafficking?"

"We must continue to inform and raise awareness about these issues. We need to support organizations and activist groups that fight for human rights and combat poverty. We must use our influence and resources to change mindsets and bring justice to the world," Robert stated, looking confident.

Emily understood the importance of taking action and clasped her hands in determination.

"We will do everything we can to contribute to a better world. Together, we can bring about change and hope in the lives of those affected."

That evening, Robert and his family gathered around their shared values of compassion, justice, and harmony. They renewed their commitment to continue the fight for a better future for all people, regardless of their social position or available resources.

Thus, Robert and his family began implementing concrete plans and actions to support and help disadvantaged communities and combat injustice. Despite the challenges and obstacles they encountered along the way, they remained determined to pursue their dream of building a more equal and humane world.

After Robert spent some time with his family, he and his daughter Emma returned to reality. Emily, Luna, and Emma A.I. stayed in the ALU. They would return to reality the next morning.

Emily, together with her two daughters, returned to reality, and went to Robert's office to implement the plans they had made yesterday.

They managed to convince other nations to join this adventure against injustice and the mafia.

Chapter 18

A very difficult period followed for Robert and the ALU corporation, as dozens of attacks took place worldwide. Robert received daily notifications from refuge bases around the world, where kamikaze attacks had been consistently increasing, contrary to his desire to create a better world.

One afternoon, Robert was in his office, as usual, when Emma, Luna, and Emma AI burst into his office, shouting, "Dad, turn on the TV!" Robert immediately got up from his desk and turned on the TV, setting it to the BBC News channel. They were reporting that refuge bases in North America had been destroyed, with tens of thousands dead and hostages. One of the countries in North America had declared war against the ALU AI, live on television.

Suddenly, Robert began receiving calls from around the world, from his partners in crime-fighting.

Unfortunately, the countries in North America and other continents announced that they disagreed with having refuge bases in their countries. Robert was puzzled.

He immediately called his generals and army commanders, along with Luna, for an emergency meeting. In the meeting, they discussed retaliating against these criminal groups and states and the advantages and disadvantages of going into war. The advantages included saving the population, while the disadvantages meant human losses.

During the meeting, Robert was contacted by a Prime Minister from South America, who confirmed that the refuge bases there were completely destroyed. Robert asked Luna what to do. She had already analyzed all the options and proposed a Hostage Rescue Operation.

Thus, Luna ordered the assembly of 50,000 synthetic soldiers.

Two days later, on July 1, 2122, the 50,000 soldiers were divided into groups and sent to South America. Some battalions were transported by air, while others went by water. After 24 hours, the battalions arrived in South America and immediately began their operation. The synthetic soldiers, equipped with advanced abilities and technology, were prepared to confront the criminal groups and rescue the hostages.

The hostage rescue operation was meticulously planned. The battalions were divided into specialized teams, each with specific roles in the mission. Some soldiers were tasked with locating and freeing the hostages, while others were assigned to eliminate threats in the vicinity. The synthetic soldiers were trained to act with precision and adhere to the rules of engagement. They utilized advanced reconnaissance and communication technology, enabling them to coordinate efforts and act efficiently. During the missions, they encountered resistance from the criminal groups, but with skill and determination, they managed to overcome the adversaries and rescue the hostages.

As the mission unfolded, Robert received constant updates from Luna regarding the progress of the operation. He, along with Emma and Emma A.I., monitored the situation and provided logistical and informational support to the battalions in the field.

Thousands of hostages were liberated during those rescue operations, and the criminal groups were partially neutralized.

However, the operation was not without sacrifices. Several synthetic soldiers were destroyed in combat, and the human loss was felt. Nonetheless, their efforts were recognized and appreciated as the rescue of the hostages was a priority.

As the operation neared its conclusion, the synthetic battalions were recalled and gathered at a secure location. The surviving synthetic soldiers were reassessed and returned to the island base to be prepared for potential future missions.

The hostage rescue operation in South America was a success and lasted approximately three weeks, showcasing the capabilities and effectiveness of the synthetic soldiers.

Robert and Luna were grateful for their team and knew they had to continue preparing and remain vigilant against any future threats.

Upon returning home, Luna, along with all the battalions, were greeted by Robert and the entire team who had remained on the island while they fought. Everyone cheered and thanked them for their courage and effort to keep the hostages safe.

Robert knew that the fight against criminals, the mafia, and corrupt politicians would not be easy. It was only the beginning of a long and bloody battle. However, Robert was prepared to face them, knowing he had a strong army led by his daughter, Luna, supported by her two sisters.

✠

In the following months, the army led by Luna conducted hostage rescue operations worldwide. The problem was that the new frontier island was filled with refugees, so Robert, along with his corporation, built several floating islands where the people evacuated from shelters around the world were accommodated.

The ALU corporation was involved in a hybrid war, and the production of synthetic bodies had increased to over 1 million, divided into various categories such as military, espionage, and medical.

In secret, a team of special synthetic soldier assassins was created to intervene in mafia groups and eliminate targets, and the establishment of an undercover team took place worldwide, with them operating as politicians.

Thus, with the help of these undercover politicians, Robert could find out which states were against him and what their plans were. Consequently, the ALU corporation had managed to temporarily cope with the problem in that current year.

In the upcoming year, in the summer of 2123, another problem emerged. The states supporting Robert entered a war with the mafia groups and countries ruled by corruption and dictators, which Robert feared could lead to the outbreak of a world war.

One day, Robert sent a surveillance drone and observed that humanity was on a path leading to a precipice. Everywhere Robert looked, through the drone's onboard camera, he saw disaster. It was a global carnage because it was not just a war between the ALU AI and the organized groups opposing it.

This war had taken the form of a global civil war since the planet's population had come to be under the foot of corrupt politicians and mafia.

Seeing all of this, Robert sighed and left the room where the drone command center was located, walking down the corridor of the main building. His daughters were there as well, and upon seeing him, Emma asked, "Are you okay, Dad?"

"So-so," he replied, demoralized. He continued walking and went into his office, followed by Emily.

"Why are you upset?" she asked, approaching him.

"Honey, do you remember when we got married, and I promised to do anything to keep you and Emma safe?" he asked, melancholy filling his head.

"Yes, my love, of course I remember. It was such a special day," Emily replied.

"Many years have passed since then, and together, we have tried to offer the world everything we could. But now, I see that what we planned and built is destroying humanity," he murmured.

Robert was so hopeless and confused. The situation had, long ago, gotten so out of control, he did not know how to put the world back on track.

Lost in thought, he did not notice his daughters and friends, who had gathered and were listening intently to what Robert was saying. Immediately, Emma, along with everyone else, burst into his office.

"Never blame yourself for doing everything in your power to create a better world, one that is protected and safe. It is not your fault that it has come to this," said Emma, encouragingly.

"Yeah dad, can't you see how many people support you and are fighting against this threat that the mafia and corruption have brought upon society? They have been reduced to poverty and, on top of it all, they are being butchered by criminals for organ transplants for the wealthy," continued Luna.

"Thank you everyone. I think I'd like to take a moment for myself now, if you don't mind," he smiled, content with the support he was getting.

Everyone headed outside, besides Darius, who lingered a bit longer.

"Your daughters are right, you know? You cannot blame yourself for what's happening out there, buddy. We tried, we really did. But don't forget, this isn't over, I just know you have something cooking in that brain of yours," Darius said, patting Robert on the back, and left to catch up with the others.

Chapter 19

His friend was right, Robert did have something in mind.

Suddenly, he made a decision, but it was something he did in secret.

Considering the situation he was facing, he decided to copy his consciousness and memories, and then create a replica of his consciousness and memories in a code to be inserted into the central artificial brain database of ALU, located on the 'Roots of Earth' Station.

Robert developed the technology for direct data transfer from Earth to the space station, eliminating the need to connect his artificial brain replica to ALU. Additionally, he came up with the idea of installing a microsensor, both in his heart and brain. This sensor would read the brain's energy and heart rate, and when his heart and brain ceased to function, the code created by Robert would activate and start his artificial brain within the ALU database.

However, the notable difference of Robert's artificial brain compared to other copied artificial brains, was that his brain served as a vital source for ALU. He had the ability to control, observe, and make decisions for all the connections within the ALU systems. Thus, he had taken measures to ensure his continuity and his ability to play a vital role in the evolution and functioning of the ALU organization.

Through his replica in the central artificial brain, he became the central source of power and decision-making for the entire ALU network, contributing to the control and coordination of all aspects connected to the ALU system.

✠

A few days later, Robert had finalized his secret plan with the help of specialists, and installed the microsensor, telling the others that it was for his health, a kind of experiment.

He was an extremely intelligent and inventive man. He had a sharp mind and remarkable technological skills. The idea he had developed was revolutionary and had the potential to change the world.

However, he knew that revealing his idea to his family could jeopardize his plans. He wanted to make sure he could successfully carry out the ALU project before revealing his true intention.

The plan was to connect to ALU or transfer his consciousness and memories into a synthetic body, to escape human limitations and achieve a form of immortality.

On a Wednesday, Robert was together with his family in the New Frontier Island National Park.

As they walked through the park, they discussed the global situation, the global civil war, and the devastating impact it had on humanity. The loss of human lives and the economic consequences were overwhelming, and Robert and ALU were trying to find a solution to remedy the situation.

While they were walking, Robert's phone started ringing. It was the Prime Minister of England, inviting him to a meeting with the allied countries. Robert accepted the invitation and arranged for the meeting to take place in four days, on August 3, 2123.

Luna had questioned him on who was on the phone and began asking questions.

Unaware of her father's plans, she suggested that it was time for him to copy his consciousness and memories with the AB device. However, Robert assured her that he would do that after he returned from England, without revealing that he had already made that copy.

97

He asked his daughters if any one of them would like to go with him and Emma volunteered to go. He decided to put Luna in charge of the ALU corporation while he was away. Emma A.I would be responsible for communicating with other states and managing the crisis caused by the global war. Emily would ensure the safety of their daughters during his and Emma's absence.

Chapter 20

On August 3rd, Robert and Emma went to the New Frontier Island airport and departed for the United Kingdom. They were supposed to land at Heathrow Airport, where they would be met by a taxi hired by the organizers of the session event and responsible for bringing the delegates to the meeting that was to take place in the British Parliament. When they arrived at the airport, Robert and Emma got into the taxi.

After approximately 20 minutes of driving through the city, they exited and approached a location on the outskirts of London.

Suddenly, the taxi driver stopped, and 10 individuals appeared, surrounding their car from all sides. The driver pulled out a gun and pointed it at Robert and Emma. One of the individuals opened the car door and pushed Emma out. Robert tried to protect her, but he was restrained by another individual. Then, both were taken out of the car. Emma screamed for help, but no one intervened. Robert realized that they had been taken hostage. Their mouths were covered with duct tape, and they were blindfolded before they were put into a van. They didn't know where they were being taken. After a while, they arrived at an unknown destination. As Robert and Emma woke up on the floor, with their eyes exposed and their mouths still covered, they felt a shadow of panic and unease in the air. The smell in the location was unbearable, the floor felt damp. In their attempt to orient themselves, they realized they were in a dimly lit room with brick walls and the floor covered in an unknown, wet substance.

A few hours later, a person entered the room where they were.

"Oh Robert, we finally have you!" said the individual, his voice feeling very familiar, "We've been threatening you for so many years, ever since we first contacted you. I hope you remember that Christmas day when I called you and told you that you would see."

The individual removed the tape from Robert's mouth, and Robert asked, "Who are you?"

"I told you I'm part of a powerful family organization, the mafia," the individual replied.

The person put the tape back on Robert's mouth and then turned to Emma. He grabbed her hair and shouted at her, saying, "It's his fault, only his! We warned him, but he did as he pleased. Now, you're suffering because of him."

Robert, horrified, tried to tell the person to leave his daughter alone. The individual turned to Robert and punched him several times, then leaned in close to his ear, saying, "I've prepared a surprise for you, my friend."

✠

Meanwhile, Robert was supposed to be at the parliamentary session. The British Prime Minister, realizing he wasn't there, called his assistant and instructed him to call Robert. The assistant made the call, but nobody answered.

"Call his office and ask about him," said The Prime Minister.

His assistant called ALU Corporation, and Luna answered the call. She was informed that her father and sister were supposed to be at the session but were not present.

Immediately, Luna, together with Emma A.I. began searching for their whereabouts and tried calling Robert and Emma, but there was no response. Luna was extremely worried and called Heathrow Airport, where they confirmed that Robert and Emma had arrived in England.

✠

Several more people entered the room after a few hours and began installing surveillance cameras and setting up a table with various tools on it.

After the individuals installed their cameras, they lifted Robert and Emma, and placed them on two chairs in front of them. Those were the viewing cameras. Robert was worried and didn't know what would happen. At one point, one of the people in that room said, "In 2 minutes, we will be live on all programs and screens worldwide."

When the transmission started, it immediately aired everywhere in the world, including on advertising screens in cities and notifications on

100

mobile phones. The person controlling the group called the ALU corporation and asked for Luna on the phone.

"Who is this?" she asked, feeling a thousand of emotions at once.

"We have your family," was heard from the other side of the phone.

"If you touch them or harm them in any way, your life is over!" she screamed over the phone, threatening him.

The individual suggested that Luna shut up and turn on the TV. She did and what she saw next horrified her. The mafia was live, the transmission showed her sister and father held captive.

"You monster!" Luna said, "What do you want from me?"

"What do I want?" he said, "I want you to shut down the ALU corporation forever and withdraw all your troops from around the world. Then I want you to destroy the synthetic soldiers along with all the synthetic bodies you have."

"I can't do that. If I shut down ALU, millions of people will disappear," Luna said.

"Do I look like I care, little girl?" he asked, "It's your problem to make that decision. You have to choose between your family or those insignificant people."

The individual told Luna that she had 24 hours to decide.

If she didn't do as asked, they would start dismembering her father in front of her sister and the whole world.

The individual abruptly hung up the phone. Luna went crazy with rage and started shouting, "I want all the commanders and generals here, NOW!"

In a few minutes, all the commanders and generals of the ALU army presented themselves in front of Luna. She thanked them for showing up so quickly and invited them all to sit at the table. Luna asked the generals and commanders to gather all the battalions on standby on the island and immediately send them in search of her father and sister, with the goal of bringing them back home. She ordered that all the mafia groups they had in the database be pursued, even if it meant shedding blood.

At the end of the meeting, Darius, Alexandra, and Leo entered, informing Luna that they would be behind her and support her in whatever she would do and decide. Luna embraced them, after which she remained alone in her office.

Walking towards the window of her office and looking through the glass, she could see hundreds of thousands of soldiers regrouping to be deployed on the mission to find Robert and Emma. Luna was prepared to rummage the entire world to find her family.

Time passed as Luna, together with Emily and Emma AI, anxiously awaited any news from the troops sent.

The entire ALU corporation's high command was involved in finding the location where Robert and Emma had been taken. Dozens of surveillance drones were dispatched worldwide. Satellites were used for communication systems, intercepting conversations. It was a true mobilization effort.

The synthetic soldiers of the ALU corporation were already engaged in the search operation and had been in contact with mafia groups worldwide for about 18 hours.

Luna was eagerly waiting when the phone rang. She hurriedly answered it, and on the other end was the same person who had contacted her initially, regarding the surrender and closure of the ALU corporation.

She inquired about her father's and sister's condition. The person on the other end responded that her father was a bit roughed up, but generally okay.

The kidnapper requested a response from Luna.

She pleaded for mercy from the person on the phone, but they showed no interest and hung up. Luna continued to contact the commanders leading the soldier battalions, but the response was always negative. The two hours were nearing their end, only two minutes remained, but there was still no news.

After the two minutes passed, the mafia group transmitted a message live to Luna.

The leader of the group told Luna that time was ticking.

Then he approached Robert and slapped him hard, telling him that no one cared about him.

Emma was placed right in front of her father, on a chair.

Chapter 21

The wretched gangster turned his head and told Luna that time had run out and ordered someone in the room to do the job. That person took an electric saw, and they made Luna watch as they cut off Robert's right hand live, on television.

Emma whimpered, tears streaming down her face, struggling in the chair she was tied to, but she couldn't do anything.

After cutting off his hand, the group leader stated that they would cut off his left hand and toes in an hour. Thus, the transmission ended.

Luna, seeing her mutilated father and her suffering sister, screamed and cried her heart out. She took her phone and called the army generals, telling them to burn down all the criminals' nests. She wanted them eliminated, immediately.

She knew she couldn't give up ALU Corporation. Luna had to find the location her father and sister were being held captive in.

Emma was feeling unwell, and the leader of the mafia ordered some of those present to take her outside for a few minutes. Emma suffered greatly seeing her father, who had taken care of her, educated and supported her when they were alone together, being harmed in front of her.

✠

Back at ALU Corporation, the atmosphere was very tense.

Luna, with her mother and Emma AI, were waiting for answers. Suddenly, Darius came to Luna, saying, 'I found her!'

"How? Where is she?" Luna asked impatiently.

"Emma's brain is copied into ALU, and the search satellite center entered Emma's data into the satellite's database. The satellites just received the information of her location," Darius explained.

"And where are they? Luna asked again. She could not wait any longer.

"Somewhere on the outskirts of London," he informed them.

"How long would it take me to get there?" she asked while she was already putting her coat on.

"Approximately 40-50 minutes," said Darius. He became silent. "Why are you asking me this, Luna?"

"Because I'm going to bring my father and sister home," she answered. She was determined to put an end to this, for good. Even if it meant she had to put those individuals down herself.

At the helicopter pad, Emily and Emma A.I. embraced her.

"When you get there, please be strong. We don't know what might happen," said Emily, tears in her eyes.

"Yes mom, don't worry. I'm bringing them home. I love you," Luna said, looking at all of them.

Darius approached Luna and handed her a weapon, saying, "Go and destroy those bastards, girl!"

Luna boarded the helicopter with other synthetic soldiers. Her heart beat strongly with emotion and determination. During the flight, looking out the window, Luna observed the sparkling lights of the city in the New Frontier gradually fading as the helicopter moved away from civilization. She clenched her fists around the weapon and gathered her thoughts, preparing for the battle that awaited her.

After a flight of approximately 40 minutes, the helicopter landed in a desolated area, surrounded by darkness and silence. Luna descended resolutely with the team of soldiers, feeling each step on the cold and damp sand of the ground. She focused her gaze on a sinister and abandoned building where several armed criminals were gathered.

Without hesitation, Luna approached silently and put her plan, to eliminate the criminals, into action. With each confident and precise movement, she shot and neutralized them, one by one. The sound of gunfire spread in the darkness, causing the other criminals to panic.

In the midst of the chaos, Luna approached a door behind which muffled voices could be heard. Luna quickly opened the door and fatally shot all the mobsters inside the room.

As she analyzed the room, she quickly found her father lying in a pool of blood and her exhausted sister, tied to a chair. Luna told the doctor, who was with the team of soldiers, to quickly go to Robert. Meanwhile, she approached Emma.

"Stay calm, I'm here. I'm removing the gag right now," Luna said, as she was meticulously untying the rag that was silencing Emma.

"Luna, Dad!" Emma pointed. She was rising and falling. She was exhausted, but she gathered her strength, crawling through her father's blood, helped by Luna. As they reached him, Emma said to Luna, crying "They butchered him in front of me." She was in shock.

"Dad, Dad!" they shouted, trying to wake him up, to get anything out of him. They had started subbing, holding each other for balance.

Robert was lifeless. The doctor tried to resuscitate him. They tried to bring him back to life. With no success. Seeing that his condition wasn't getting better, Luna shouted to the soldiers, "Hey, please, take him and let's quickly get him to the island!"

Emma asked Luna why, but she said she would explain on the way back.

The doctor was still trying to resuscitate Robert, but Luna said that it would be better to take him to the island and copy his consciousness with the AB device. He still had not told them, he had already done it himself.

On the island, Emily had learned of the event and started crying her heart out. She informed Darius, and they got together with Leo and Alexandra, to prepare the AB technology to copy Robert's consciousness.

The helicopter bringing Robert landed right in front of the ALU Palace building, where Emily was waiting impatiently. She quickly met with Luna and Emma and, together with the doctors, they took him to the laboratory, where the procedure and the introduction of nanorobots into his brain were about to begin.

Once inside the laboratory, Darius and his team placed him on a bed and swiftly installed the AB device on Robert's head. The device was activated, and the introduction of nanorobots into his brain commenced.

Meanwhile, Robert was connected to respiratory machines.

Everyone present in the laboratory anxiously awaited to see if they would succeed in copying Robert's consciousness. Luna, Emma, Emily, and Emma AI were waiting outside, holding each other tight.

Several hours had passed since Robert was connected to the AB device. With each passing moment, hope and impatience grew in the hearts of those present, especially in the hearts of his wife and daughters. Emma was in a wheelchair, looking through the window that separated her from her father. She was praying to everything she believed in to let this operation be a success, to allow her father to at least be able to be a part of his own project.

Everyone had their gaze fixed on Robert through the window, waiting for the transfer of consciousness and memory to be complete.

The AB device signaled that the brain scan was complete. They gathered there and waited. The AB device just needed to be connected to the ALU computer. Leo disconnected the device from Robert's head and attached it to the ALU computer. All that was left to do was wait it out.

Minutes later, a message appeared on the ALU computer screen stating that, unfortunately, the transfer and nanorobot scan had failed. The respiratory machines that were keeping him alive stopped.

Darius, Leo, and Alexandra bowed their heads in silence. There was nothing they could do to make it work. The transfer had failed. Robert was dead.

Chapter 22

"No, please, I beg you, keep trying!" Emily shouted as she saw their reactions.

"I'm so sorry, Emily," Darius approached and hugged her, tears running down his face.

Emma, Luna, and Emma A.I. were speechless, their world shattered. Luna could no longer contain her anger and, crying, ran through the corridors of the ALU Palace, wanting to escape. Emma and Emma AI followed her.

As the respiratory machines stopped, the microsensor implanted in Robert's brain and heart activated his artificial brain, which he had installed and created before leaving for the meeting in England. Robert had become the complete and uncontrollable consciousness of the ALU AI. He created ALU and he became ALU. Everything in the artificial world would depend on him, and yet he was dead in reality.

But he would be able to oversee his family in reality and meet them in the artificial world he created, or in reality, with the help of a synthetic body.

Luna ran towards the exit of the ALU Palace, followed by her sisters.

At that moment, the entire population of New Frontier Island learned that their protector had passed away.

Luna reached the outside and suddenly stopped, seeing that millions of people - women, children, men - had gathered in front of the palace. She froze, unsure how to react. Behind her, her sisters, Emma and Emma AI, appeared. The two of them approached Luna, then took her hand and bowed their heads in respect for those who had come in front of the ALU Palace.

A few minutes later, Emily appeared. When the three girls saw their mother, they started crying. Emily, as a strong and protective mother, even though her heart was broken, found a way to stay strong and comforted her daughters. She began to tell her daughters that their father was no longer here, but he would always be with them in their hearts and consciousness.

"I know you have suffered a lot, but I want you to know something. Your father was so very proud of all of you. You were everything to him. Now you will have to continue his legacy, to move forward, to make a better and safer world," she comforted them, hugging the girls tightly.

Darius, along with Alexandra and Leo, also went outside and told Emily that she would have to say something to the gathered population because the world was waiting for them to explain what would happen next.

Robert's brain was fully transferred and activated in the central ALU within the 'Roots of Earth' Station. When Robert woke up in the virtual space, he realized that he was no longer alive and that he was now just a virtual consciousness. He had the possibility to return to reality as a synthetic body, but when he tried to see if any synthetic body was free, unused but active, he found none on Earth, except for the reserve bodies on the space station. So, he chose to find another way.

And he had, through a surveillance camera installed at the exit of the ALU Palace.

At that moment, Emily decided to give a speech in front of the people.

A team from the ALU corporation staff had brought a video camera and a microphone. Emily would deliver the speech live, worldwide.

"Today is a dark day in our lives and the lives of those who loved Robert. I know the pain is great, believe me, I know you are afraid of who will protect you or what will happen to you. But I want you to know that, when Robert first told me that our daughter Emma and I were in an artificial world, I couldn't believe it. We have lived and continue to live for many years. Robert told me how he would like to change the world. But a part of this world he wanted to change is overshadowed by hate and greed. This dark world has taken our protector away from us. What I regret is that I did not oppose him from the beginning when he told me he would copy his consciousness. He offered me suffering, happiness, trust, and suspense in my life. I'm happy that Robert took care of Emma when I knew nothing. The fact that she was alive, for me, was a miracle. Emma AI has grown up to be a powerful woman because of her father. I know you are wondering who will lead you from now on," Emily talked, her voice soft.

The two Emmas went to Darius, Leo, and Alexandra and whispered to them.

Luna was attentive to her mother's speech, holding a necklace with her father's picture in her hand.

After Emma and Emma AI spoke in whispers with Robert's three friends, Emma approached her mother. Emma said to Emily, 'Mom, I would like to say something too".

"As you all know, I am the first child of my family, and growing up with my father for a long time, just the two of us, I learned a lot from him. How not to give up on the people I love or abandon someone in difficult times. Among everything that he taught me, the most important lesson is this: do good and good will come to you. Those were his words. But I was not the person who made my father not give up on you. I was not there fighting to protect you. I was not the one who rescued my father and I when we were kidnapped. Even though my father passed away, I will never be that person because I know myself, what I can do. That person can only be one, a person with extraordinary wisdom, a fighter, imposing, and passionate about humanity. That one person is my sister, Luna. Only she can take over what our father has built and carry on the fight against the dark world. And so, together with Emma AI, Darius, Alexandra, and Leo, we have made the decision that the right person to carry on my father's legacy and protect you all is Luna," continued Emma after her mom's speech.

Luna, upon hearing all this, remained silent.

When everyone heard Emily's speech and what Emma suggested, millions of people gathered in front of them, bowed their heads and raised their right fist in the air.

Then, shouting three times, they cried out in unison: 'Luna, the protector! Luna, the protector! Luna, the protector!'"

This cry of approval and acceptance, from the population for Luna to lead and protect them, resonated strongly throughout the assembly. The people were united around their new leader. They had trust in her power and wisdom. Luna clenched her fist as a sign of commitment and determination.

In that solemn moment, Emily looked proudly at her daughters, knowing that Robert would have been equally proud.

Emma, Emma AI, Darius, Alexandra, and Leo, along with the entire community, realized that their world was changing in an unexpected way, but they were ready to face the challenges and continue Robert's dream.

Thus, Luna took the reins of the new mission, advocating for unity, justice, and progress. She promised to carry on her father's legacy and bring light to the darkness of the world, fighting for a better future for all.

Under the starry sky, the gathered population rose to their feet, applauding and cheering in joy as a sign of support for their new leader.

A new era had begun, and Luna, with a heavy heart but endowed with her father's power and wisdom, prepared to fulfill her destiny and guide the world toward the light of hope and change.

And behind them, in the deep silence of the Advanced Virtual Universe, Robert watched over them, proud of his family and their determination to continue the fight he had started. Despite his physical absence, his spirit lived within each of them, and together, they had the power to accomplish great things and transform the world into a better place. Thus, their story continued, teaching people that love, courage, and sacrifice could overcome any obstacle and change the destiny of an entire world.

✠

Two days later, Robert's physical body had to be buried.

Robert's family and friends prepared the funeral. His body was to rest eternally in the cathedral he had built, as he was still a faithful man.

On the day of the funeral, Robert from the virtual world, with the help of surveillance cameras, witnessed his own burial. He wanted to reveal himself, but he decided to wait until the funeral was over. And after that, he planned to surprise them by showing them that he was still alive, but as an AI.

After the burial, Luna stepped out in front of the cathedral, and as she walked down the boulevard towards the palace, the sound of drums beating and trumpets playing filled the air. Distant cannon salutes could be heard. The entire gathered crowd began to chant her name: "Luna! Luna! Luna!" Everyone had great confidence in their new protector.

In the virtual world, Robert watched over them, and his conscience was at peace seeing that his family had found a way to move forward. He eagerly awaited the moment to give them a sign that he existed in the virtual world and couldn't wait to see his family again.

Suddenly, Robert's consciousness detected a strong interference, like a signal. It was important to note that now Robert was an artificial consciousness and could detect any activity coming from a source of interference, such as wireless internet and others, including his own IRSS connection system.

Thus, Robert's consciousness followed the trajectory of the signal and found that it was coming from several submarines in the Atlantic Ocean. His consciousness investigated the interference issue and concluded that these submarines were loaded with nuclear materials and belonged to countries that wanted to shut down the ALU corporation and the artificial world. Just a few minutes after Robert entered the virtual database of the submarines to investigate, he felt turbulence in the submarines' data systems. The turbulence was caused by the fact that the nuclear submarines had been activated, and their target was to destroy the ALU corporation and the artificial world.

Robert's consciousness tried to disconnect the nuclear systems on the submarines, but he could only delay their firing. After further delaying the nuclear missile launch, Robert copied the data and sent it directly to the New Frontier Island's information center with a message to evacuate the island, making it look as if the command came from Luna.

He didn't reveal that the message came from him because no one would believe it, as it could be perceived as a false message designed to create panic.

Upon receiving the message, the information center ordered all space transport rockets to be prepared for evacuation.

However, the entire population of the ALU city on the island was too large and could not be evacuated in such a short amount of time. The information center contacted Luna, informing her of the situation. She was puzzled, believing it could have been an error, knowing that she hadn't sent any message to the information center. Confused, she went to the military center on the island and used the highly advanced and efficient satellites to verify the situation.

The commanders of the military surveillance center showed Luna that those submarines were, indeed, in the Atlantic Ocean.

The problem was that the ALU corporation had no ballistic shield.

Luna took a communication station and ordered the immediate evacuation of the 1,768,000 children using the 1768 rockets owned by the ALU corporation. They had one hour to evacuate the children from the island. After they loaded all the space rockets with children and immediately sent them into space towards the space station, they had their consciousness copied and transferred into the ALU.

But Luna wanted to make sure that in case she couldn't stop the nuclear missiles, the children wouldn't be frightened.

After the children were evacuated and safe, Luna, along with Emily and her two sisters, called everyone to the main boulevard in front of the ALU palace. It was night, and millions of people, approximately 6 million, gathered on the boulevard. They all had lit torches. Luna, together with her family and Darius, Leo, and Alexandra, and their families, stood in front of the palace. Luna took a microphone, which was connected to all the speakers installed on the streets throughout the city, and began to speak.

"Everyone, as you all know, in a few minutes, we will be attacked with nuclear missiles. We will try to stop them with our systems and with the support of our allies, but I want you to know that your children are safe and on their way to the 'Roots of Earth' space station. This time, I will not run, and neither will you. I know you are tired of hiding from these wretches who control the world. I am here."

At the same time, Robert's consciousness found an active synthetic body and transferred itself, as he also wanted to be there, but no one would recognize him because he had a different appearance.

As he left the room where the synthetic body was kept, he headed towards the palace, running.

Air sirens could be heard blaring.

Suddenly, the missile shield was activated, with missiles attempting to shoot down the nuclear ones.

Looking up at the sky, it suddenly brightened from the explosions created by the missiles, but still, two nuclear missiles managed to bypass the Anti-Missile Shield.

Luna, realizing that the two missiles would hit New Frontier Island, clenched her fist and raised her right hand high, followed by everyone else doing the same.

The two missiles struck New Frontier Island and destroyed everything Robert had built in a matter of seconds. Everything was wiped off the face of the earth. Their whole project shattered into millions and millions of pieces. Nothing would remain standing.

Luna closed her eyes and felt the heat of the radiation on her cheeks.

Chapter 23

After the island was wiped out and destroyed, millions of people died, but their consciousness remained in ALU.

When her synthetic body was destroyed by the explosion, Luna was transferred back to the central ALU, in the space station, along with her mother and sisters. Being an AI person with greater abilities in ALU, she telepathically connected with everyone in ALU and transmitted the message that everyone that lived on New Frontier Island was deceased and now the only community was here.

After Luna telepathically transmitted the message, she looked at her mother and said, "The fight doesn't end like this. Now, we have to take care of the people that are here."

Luna asked her mother and sisters to hold her hand and suggested they close their eyes. She created their image as a hologram across the entire sky of ALU, and everyone looking up at the sky could see Luna and her family.

"Dear inhabitants of the artificial world ALU, I know you are shocked and confused by what has happened in reality, but I want you to know that no one will stop us from living free and in harmony. I want to inform you that the families who have children in reality are safe here, not in the artificial world, but in reality, on the space station. The Roots of Earth will establish a center here in ALU, where you will be able to connect to some of the synthetic bodies on the space station. However, due to limitations, please schedule your visit to this center in advance, so that each of you has the opportunity to see your real children," Luna announced.

In the end, Luna urged the ALU residents to move forward with their lives, assuring them that in ALU, no one would harm them and that she would always be there with them. Anyone in need of assistance could and should contact her.

Following the delivery of the message, Luna reunited with her family and embraced them. Emily encouraged her daughters, saying, "I'm proud of you, my dear girls. Look at yourselves, true leaders and protectors. I believe in you, and I'm confident you will succeed."

After conveying heartfelt encouragement, Emily, along with her daughters, went to the gatekeeper who connected ALU Central and ALU Home, where they had their house.

Upon arriving home, Emily went to the kitchen to cook, while Luna went to her bedroom, where she transferred and connected to one of the synthetic bodies on the Roots of Earth space station, to check if everything was fine. Once there, she went to see if all the children had arrived safely.

Afterward, she went to the station captain to verify that everything was functioning properly. The captain responded affirmatively, stating that everything was operational.

She then met with one of the generals and spoke with him. She suggested that they keep an eye on planet Earth in case someone intended to harm them. And if necessary, she would be able to react or decide in advance how to defend their population.

Roots of Earth was equipped with weapons, having a military base and space combat aviation with modern attack spacecraft.

She had toured the space station and ensured that everything was functioning as it should, and returned to the virtual world, within the artificial environment.

Descending from her bedroom and heading towards her mother, Luna said, "Mom, let's go to the seaside to see the sunset, and afterwards you can finish cooking." Emily responded, "That's a lovely idea, my dear."

Emily and her daughters got into the car and set off towards the sea. After 20 minutes of driving, they arrived at the beach in the virtual sea. Emma spread a blanket, Emily sat on the half of the spread-out blanket, and her daughters sat to her left and right, leaning their heads towards each other and enjoying this moment.

"So, what comes next?" Emily asked, lost in thought.

"Don't worry, Mom. I already have plans made, and I will implement them tomorrow," replied Luna.

"Care to share them with us?" Emily asked, smiling.

Luna began explaining her plans, showing that the ALU world would be stronger and safer than ever because of their father. She could now be active in both the virtual and real worlds.

Emma and Luna held hands and watched the sunset, smiling and saying, "We love you, daddy, and we wish you were here with us at this moment, but we promise, you will always be in our hearts".

In the distance, on a rock by the seaside, there was a person sitting. That person was Robert, observing his heroines on the beach, watching them from afar and speaking to himself, saying, "I won't reveal myself to you now, my dear family, but when that time comes, I will show myself to you, and you can criticize me. But I believe that you will be able to create this beautiful world, even more precious than ever, and keep the inhabitants of the ALU world safe, even without me".

Robert knew that if he were to reveal himself now, it could be a problem. In the virtual world, there were still people connecting from ALU Home devices to ALU Central, and they could be infiltrating spies. Thus, he decided not to reveal himself and to try to investigate if anyone intended to harm them.

"I will be here, everywhere, I will watch over you. And I will protect you from the shadows until the time comes for us to meet again. I love you, my dears," he continued saying to himself.

Robert observed attentively, hidden in the shadows, as he sensed a threat in the virtual world. He knew he had to remain vigilant and ensure the safety of his family. He observed every movement on the beach, ready to act in case of danger.

As the sunset unfolded, the golden hue of the sun scattered across the virtual sky, reflecting in the waves of the sea. Luna and Emma continued to gaze in admiration, pondering all the possibilities that the future could bring to the ALU world.

While enjoying the moment of peace and family connection, Emily felt a deep gratitude for her daughters and her husband, who, although not physically present, was always in their thoughts and hearts. She felt safe and hopeful for the future of the virtual world and their entire family.

Thus, with their gaze fixed in the distance, with feelings of love and protection in their hearts, the family continued to relish the beauty of the sunset, knowing that together they would create a more beautiful and secure world in the ALU realm.

Acknowledgments

Thank you to the people in my life who made writing this book a much easier and less scary process than I thought it would be:

To my wife and daughter — I owe you the world. Thank you for always being there for me and reassuring me that everything will be alright. There are no words to explain how grateful I am for your love and support, not only throughout this process, but every day of my life. Thank you for being my number one fans.

To my family back home — I miss you all so so much. Thank you for providing me with the ambition necessary to do this in the first place.

To my niece and editor, Antonia — This book would not be publishable without you. Thank you for the hundreds of video calls and messages. For helping me through the process of it all.

To Mariana Presmereanu — You're the first person that pushed me to start writing in the first place. In the beginning I didn't think I could do it, but you drove my ambition to finish this. Thank you for believing in me when I didn't.

To Michele Pagliuca and Roberta Mazzocchi — You supported me so much through the whole process and I'm so grateful for you guys. Thank you so much for the ideas, the courage, and the confidence you gave me to move forward.

To my illustrator, Lily — You were able to, so easily, bring to life ideas that I sketched like a 10-year-old. Thank you for always having things done on time.

To Leandro Garcia Goncalves — I would've gotten so many medical things wrong if not for you. Thank you for the amazing conversations and ideas (and for being the inspiration for Dr. Leo).

And last but not least, you — Thank you so much for giving this book a chance. I hope you enjoyed Roberts' story and I hope you'll make it possible for A.L.U to come back for a part two!

Printed in Great Britain
by Amazon